LOVE ME, NOT DESTROY ME

LUCAS AND AMELIA

MJ MANGO

ISBN: 9798334182448

Cover by: Grim Whimsy

❀ Created with Vellum

To Kinlei, my inspiration for little Riley. Her sassiness and funny play with words have always been adorable to everyone that meets her.

To my Nicholas and London, because a part of their bossiness and speech is mixed in with Kinlei's.

Together, they've given me the sweetest little girl that has become one of the best parts of this story.

CHAPTER 1

melia

FOREST VIEW MOUNTAINS, a place that has never been good to me, not even as a child. So, the fact that I'm back here, after swearing never to come back, has me a bit pissed off.

Actually, pissed off doesn't even begin to describe how I feel when it comes to being back in my hometown. I'm also terrified to face some truths that I hoped to never have to face. Now it seems that I have no choice.

I left here five years ago with a broken heart and a plan to make a name for myself. Not only did I want to make my mother proud, I wanted to show all of the assholes in this town that I was more than what they saw in me. I wanted to show them that I wasn't the poor, naïve, nerdy little girl that they swore I was.

I didn't get along with many of the children I went to school with. To them, I was too quiet, too timid. I was a nuisance to some and an obstacle to others. It didn't help that

I was the cliché nerd with bushy hair and thick glasses. It also didn't help that I didn't have much growing up.

My mother was a single mother who worked as a nanny for a wealthy family, the MacArthurs. The MacArthurs were a nice family and paid my mother pretty decently, but she was doing everything on her own.

Marie MacArthur, the mother, was a pediatrician and her husband, Evan, was a surgeon. Although they worked a lot, they always made time for their children, and when they weren't around they made sure that someone was there to love them. That's where my mother came in. She worked for them for as long as I can remember.

I remember as a little girl getting up early so my mother could be there when the children woke up. When that became too much, the MacArthurs had a place built on their property for my mother and me. We stayed there throughout the rest of my school years. My mother still lives in that home, which brings me to my current problem.

My life will soon change forever, and there is nothing I can do about it. I tried to stay away and never come back to this place. I really did, but my mother's been sick recently so I was summoned home.

As you can imagine, over the years my mother has become quite close with Mrs. MacArthur. So when she contacted me about my mother, she didn't do so as an employer but as a friend. She gave me two options. Either I came home willingly or she would come find me and drag me back with her.

"Amelia, I don't know why you choose to stay away. I won't question you, but your mother needs you. She's been needing you, wanting to lay her eyes on you and not just talk to you on a phone. Whatever your issue is, you will get over it and come see your mother. I expect you no later than two days from now or I'm coming to you."

Everything she said hurt my heart. I have a wonderful mother, and I never wanted to hurt her. She absolutely deserved more than I could give but in my mind, it would hurt her more to know my life isn't what she worked so hard for it to be.

Nothing that I have done since I left will make my mother proud. I didn't finish school, I don't have an amazing career, and I'm living no better than we did when she was struggling. None of it matters now though because she needs me.

So, here I am, heading down the highway to a place I hate, to a home that I used to love, to a mother that I missed and couldn't see, but most of all, to the man that not only broke my heart but is also the father to my little girl, Lucas MacArthur.

Lucas MacArthur was what you would call the cliché popular boy in school. His parents were wealthy, he played sports, he was also really smart, and God, handsome isn't even worthy enough to be used to describe him. Lucas looked like God designed him with perfection in mind.

That's what he was to everyone else, but to me, he was the boy that I grew up with. He was the little boy that played Barbies with me while I played cars with him.

He was the little boy that begged his parents on weekends for me to stay the night, and I did until we were too old to sleep in the same bed together and it still be innocent. He was the boy that I binged all my shows with. He was my best friend, and I was secretly in love with him.

Of course, I never told him, because why would I? I thought that there was no way that a guy like him would want to date someone like me. Sure, we were friends and did a lot together but that's different than dating someone. Dating someone requires you to actually find them attractive.

Lucas had plenty of girls falling at his feet, so why waste

time on *seeing* me, but then things changed. Lucas and I started spending more time together, and I don't mean the usual two best friends hanging out kind of time.

He took me out a few times. He seemed to look at me differently and though I was hesitant, a huge part of me was happy. I thought he was finally seeing me as more than his friend, but of course, all good things must come to an end.

I will never forget the night that Lucas broke my heart. I couldn't forget it if I tried since that was the night that we conceived our daughter...my daughter. It's hard not to think of her as ours but she didn't *belong* to Lucas, and she never will.

The night that changed my life forever was the night of mine and Lucas's graduation party. It was more so Lucas's than mine but his parents always included me, and therefore he got duped into sharing the party with me.

Parties weren't usually my thing so when I got too overwhelmed I was ready to head back home, but Lucas convinced me to take a break in his room because he didn't want me to leave yet.

When he walked me to his room, he finally did something that I have been wanting him to do for a long time. He kissed me.

Now I don't know if it was my feelings talking or the spiked punch, but with the touch of his lips I decided to throw caution out the window and let him know that I wanted more.

Things happened quickly after that, and next thing I knew, I was on his bed trembling because I was so nervous.

"Trust me, Amelia. I will never hurt you." He whispered and right there in his bed, I gave Lucas MacArthur my virginity.

I thought at that moment that it was the best moment of my life. He was so gentle with me during and after. He held me close to him afterwards until I fell asleep. I was happy and content...but then I woke up and everything changed.

I used Lucas's bathroom to freshen up before heading back out to the party. At first I couldn't find him, but then I noticed him and his friends by the pool.

All I intended on doing was telling him that I was going home for a minute and then I would be back but when I got closer I heard a part of their conversation and it made me pause.

I was stuck. My feet wouldn't move as my heart broke with every single word, the words that sent me running away from him and promising to never deal with Lucas MacArthur again.

When I think about that moment it's like I can hear the words. It takes me right back to that moment where Lucas was talking to a few of his friends, one of them being Bryce Wallace.

I've personally never liked Bryce. He was always an asshole and a slut with girls which I thought was completely opposite from Lucas.

The group of them stood there talking about girls and the way they *had* them. They talked about all the girls that Lucas has had himself. Then Bryce said, "I see you finally got little Amelia to give it up."

"What did you say?" Lucas asked.

Then Bryce went into his pocket and pulled out a $100 bill and handed it to Lucas. "Here, man. I got to admit, I didn't think it was going to happen which is why I bet you a whole $100 but you actually got her to fuck you."

I couldn't listen to them anymore. I turned around and ran home as fast as I could, taking my broken heart with me. I wasn't special to Lucas. I was just another task that he fulfilled. No, actually I was less than that. I was a fucking bet to him.

I cried for hours in my room, and when I finally stopped crying I promised myself that I would never talk with him again. He called and came over, but I avoided him at all costs.

I knew he was staying close to home for college, so I made plans to go away. Within a month I was leaving home to move to a new town, and I did it when I knew that he or his family wouldn't be around.

My mother tried her best to get me to talk to her, but I wasn't going to talk about Lucas. I told her what happened, and I wouldn't talk about it again.

My plan was to stay focused on school and come back eventually when I was over him but then I started to feel sick. One trip to the emergency room for what I thought was a severe virus turned into me being pregnant.

I love my little girl, but I would be a liar if I said that I was excited about the pregnancy. I was 18 years old and had just run away from home to avoid her father. I had a small savings from earnings I made at a part-time job and the money I got from graduation. What was I going to do with a baby?

My first instincts told me to run back to Lucas. Even if I was just a random fuck to him, his family would insure that he took care of his child and be in her life, but I decided to wait. I wanted to give myself time to process everything. I wanted time to heal and be stronger when I called him.

A few days lead to a few weeks, a few weeks lead to a month, and the next thing I knew I was five months pregnant and still hadn't called Lucas. The holidays were coming up, and I knew I wouldn't be able to avoid him with this huge bump in my stomach so I decided to call him.

I called and called but there was no answer. He probably was upset that I hadn't been speaking to him, but I was within my right after what I heard. Knowing that he needed to know before I got there, I texted him.

-Hey, Lucas. I'm really sorry to text you this but I did try to call. I'm pregnant. It's yours and I know that I should have told you before now but I needed time. I will be there tomorrow and would love to talk with you about the baby. Bye.-

Needing to distract myself, I got to the task of packing my bags for the week. Once I was done, I checked my phone to see if Lucas had texted me back, and he did, but not with what I expected. I expected him to be shocked but willing to talk to me. That wasn't what I got.

-Don't text my phone anymore, Amelia. I don't know what game you're trying to run but you haven't talked to me in months. I'm not the father if you are pregnant.-

Oh, God, it still hurts to think about getting that text. Never in a million years would I have thought Lucas would say something like that. I never came home after that. I didn't have the nerve, and I wasn't about to make him be a father.

"Mommy, have to potty." Riley, my four year old, said from the backseat.

"We'll be there in about ten minutes, sweetheart. Can you hold it?" She shook her head, and I sighed heavily. "Okay. I will stop at the gas station right up the road."

A few minutes later we pulled into the gas station and rushed in. "Okay. You potty, and I will be right out here when you're done."

As much as I hated it, Riley was headstrong and independent like Lucas. She didn't like me going to the bathroom with her, because, according to her that meant she was a baby, so I stepped outside the door.

I don't know what it is, but I have to have the worst luck in the fucking world because as soon as I stepped out of the bathroom, Lucas was standing not even five feet away from me grabbing a drink from the cooler.

When he looked up, his eyes went wide. "Amelia? How

are you?" He walked towards me with his arms stretched out like he was getting ready to hug me.

I panicked and pushed myself back into the bathroom. What the hell was that about? Why would he think that I would want to be around him at all after what he said about Riley?

CHAPTER 2

ucas

WHAT IN THE actual fuck was that about? I couldn't believe my eyes when I looked up and saw Amelia. After five long years she finally decided to come back and couldn't even be decent enough to speak to me.

She acted as if I did something to her when she was the one that abandoned me and our friendship. The last time I saw or spoke to Amelia was on our graduation night five years ago.

For a long time I liked Amelia but wouldn't do anything about it because I always felt like she was too good for me. She was smart and beautiful whether she thought so or not, and I knew that she was going places. I didn't want to be the one to hold her back, so I never tried.

However, when senior year came, I decided to see where things would take us. I didn't want to regret never trying, so I took her on some dates. Then, the night of graduation happened.

I only planned on walking Amelia to my room so she could relax but when we kissed...when we kissed, the feeling of finally feeling her lips on mine was like breathing fresh air for the first time.

Our kisses lead to us making love, and it was the best feeling. The girl that has always been in my life one way or the other was finally mine, and even though we were young, I knew that I never wanted to let her go.

However, when she didn't return to the party, I went to my room to check on her only to find my bed empty. Amelia didn't talk to a lot of people because she was shy, so I assumed she decided to go home, but when the next day came I couldn't reach her no matter how hard I tried.

I have no idea what happened between us. The teenage me tortured himself over the possibility that he had rushed her to do things that she didn't want to do or that he had hurt her that night.

It took me a while to get over that and honestly, it was her mother that assured me that I hadn't hurt Amelia in that way. She still refused to tell me what was going on. I tried over and over to get a response from her but eventually I gave up. Message received, she didn't want me, but I wasn't done, because I needed to know what happened.

I knew that I could talk to her when she came home on break, but she never did. She never showed herself, not even for a day, and now she stands there in the store and acts as if I am a fucking stranger to her.

I stood there for a good ten minutes, and she still didn't come out of the bathroom. It didn't take a genius to know that she was avoiding me, but what I couldn't figure out was why.

A part of me wanted to stand there and wait until she

came out and faced me, but then what? If she didn't want me, I damn well wasn't about to make her have me.

I paid for my stuff and headed out, hating the fact that I was headed to my parents' house, because I was bound to run into Amelia, and I wasn't sure I could take too much of her running away and ignoring me before I snapped.

At least once a month on a Friday I go over and hang out at the house for the weekend. My other two adult siblings do as well. It's something that Mom insisted on when we moved out, and of course my dad backed her up.

Often times I find myself going almost every weekend. I don't have a family of my own and only casual date so spending time with them is a plus. This weekend, however, just so happened to be the fucking weekend that I am required to be there...and so would Amelia.

When I got to the house I headed straight for the four trouble makers that were the reason I went to the store anyway. My mom is strict on them about having too much junk food so here I am, once a month, sneaking in their favorite candy and snack foods from the gas station.

"Luuccaass. Did you bring the snacks?" My youngest brother Owen said.

"Hey, what no greeting, just demands? Maybe I should tell Mom what I got for you?"

"Sorry, Lucas. Hey. Did you bring the snacks?" This guy. Owen is only 10 years old, the baby of the family, and he takes his role seriously. Spoiled is an understatement, but I wouldn't change it at all.

"Yeah, I have your snacks." He hugged me like I gave him a million bucks. It's not that Mom doesn't give them snacks but considering she's a pediatrician, you can imagine how she is about our health.

The rest of the evening passed in a blur between having a family game night and playing poker with the adults. It was a much needed distraction, but it was only temporary because as soon as I wasn't busy my mind wandered to the woman that was just on the other side of the property.

That night, for the first time in years, I couldn't sleep in my parents' house. As much as I tried, sleep wouldn't find me because I couldn't stop thinking about Amelia. So, as crazy as it was, I did the thing I always did when I missed her, I walked out to the yard, right through the trees and climbed into our old clubhouse.

This place was filled with memories of two best friends that somehow had gotten to a point that they couldn't even speak to each other.

How pathetic. I'm 23 years old, sitting in a club house in the middle of the night, thinking about a woman that can't even stand my existence. The thing is, I could probably get over it if I knew why, but she didn't even think I was worthy of an explanation.

Sitting in this place, I could still hear her laughter and see her smiling. I could see us here together, playing games and sharing pizza. It was our special place. It didn't matter who else I was friends with, this was ours and ours only. I laid back and just let the memories overtake me.

My eyes fluttered open and I stretched. What the fuck? It takes me a moment to realize where I am. The last thing I remembered was thinking about Amelia. I hadn't meant to fall asleep here. I just wanted to feel a little more grounded.

Shit. Mom is going to be pissed if I miss breakfast. One thing about Marie, she does not play about her family time. I hurried and hopped out of the clubhouse and almost had a heart attack when a child screamed.

"Hey. It's okay. Are you lost?" I look at the kid, and a weird feeling overcomes me before I can even get a full view of her face.

"I not lost. Mommy say I can play til bweakfast." The little girl looked at me like I was the problem for being in my own yard, but then it hit me. A small child wouldn't wander too far so the only other option was…

"Wha-what's your mommy's name?" I don't even know why I asked. Sure, her skin is darker, and she has Amelia's dimples, but I'm looking at a female version of me.

This is my kid, mine and Amelia's, and she didn't even tell me.

CHAPTER 3

Amelia

From the previous evening.

DAY one of me being home is already going to shit. I don't know how long it took Lucas to leave the store, but I stood in that bathroom for nearly 30 minutes with Riley whining to leave.

I'm not ready to face him. What do I need to say to a man that doesn't want my child? If he didn't want me, that's fine. I'm an adult and can handle it, but Riley was innocent. She deserves her father, and to make matters worse, she's so much like him. She even looks like him.

She's nothing like me when I was younger. I was shy and a bit nerdy. This little girl of mine is headstrong and bossy. She's so smart ,but she's also adventurous. Like I said, she's all Lucas, and it's like a slap in the face.

After that little shit show at the gas station, I headed to my mother's place prepared to face the music. After all, my mother didn't know about Riley, and I was sure that she wouldn't take the news well.

Maybe it was foolish of me to hide her, but I was afraid. My mother worked hard to help me accomplish my goals, and I was afraid to disappoint her. I also was afraid that she would go to the MacArthurs about Lucas. I didn't want them to force him to be in her life. She deserves a father that wants her.

"Mommy, are we hea?" Riley asked as we parked in front of the house. I prayed and thanked God that we didn't run into anyone coming down this long path to my mother's house, because that was the last thing I needed.

"Yes, Ri. We're here. Remember to be polite, okay?"

"Mommy." She giggled. "I know to mind my mannas." She said mockingly. I couldn't help but laugh because I did say that a lot.

"Okay, little girl. Let's go meet grandma." We climbed out of the car and walked to the front door. I knocked, and it was the strangest thing. I was knocking on the door that was supposed to be home.

It took a few minutes, but my mom opened the door, and it instantly broke my heart. I could tell that she had been sick just by looking at her. I should have been here for her. I've been a horrible daughter.

"Oh, my Lord. My baby's home." She pulled me into a tight hug. "Amelia...You're home." Her voice was shaky from tears, and I hated that it was my fault that she cried. How could I be so selfish?

"Hi, Mom." I said when she leaned back and looked into my eyes, pausing to scan my face. Suddenly her attention shifted, and she noticed Riley. "Mom, this is Riley. She's... she's my daughter."

She gasped and held her chest as tears fell over her lids.

"Your…your daughter?" The shock was evident on her face as she slowly walked into the living room and sat down in her chair. "Amelia, why didn't you tell me about her?"

"I'm sorry, mom. I just…I don't know." It was a lie. I knew exactly why I didn't tell her and as soon as she knew my secret she would know too.

"Come here, sweetheart." She reached for Riley. "Such a beautiful little one." She smiled softly at Riley. When her eyes squinted I knew that she could see it. Hell, I'm surprised she didn't see it when she opened the door because the child is all him.

"She looks like…Amelia? Is she–"

"Yes. Yes, mom, she is but please don't mention it." She looked at me like I had lost my mind, and maybe I had, but for now I wouldn't talk about it. "Let's talk after Riley goes to bed, okay."

I could tell that she wanted to argue, but I was thankful when she turned to Riley instead. She took that moment to get to know Riley a little, and while I was thankful, I knew it wouldn't last.

When nighttime came, the conversation between my mom and I didn't exactly go as I thought it would. She was shocked by everything as expected but she sat there and tried to defend Lucas in front of me and it pissed me off.

Well, maybe defend isn't the right word, but she did go on and on about how she thought maybe there was a misunderstanding which I don't fucking see how. Eventually, I told her that I didn't want to deal with the conversation anymore and went off to bed with Riley.

I barely slept and it seemed like I had finally started to rest a little when Riley's little voice woke me up. "Mommy, bweakfast." The kid is an early riser, something else she doesn't get from me.

When I walk out of my old room, my mother is already

sitting at the table with her cup of coffee. "Morning, Mom." I said as I entered the kitchen. "You're up early. You don't sleep in on Saturdays anymore?"

"I do, sweetheart. I just couldn't sleep much last night." The look on her face let me know that it was because of me. Lucas has always been like a son to her, so I can understand her concern, but I don't like it.

"Do you have anything quick that I can fix Riley?" I said, brushing right over her statement about not sleeping much.

"No. You'll have to fix her something. Had I known you were coming or that–?

"Mom, please." I closed my eyes and took a long breath. "Riley, you're gonna have to be patient while I fix you something."

Riley gasped dramatically. "But I hab no patient. You said that, member?"

"I did." I sighed. "It won't take long, Ri."

"Can I play outside whiles I wait?" Definitely not a good idea. The last thing I need is for her to wander off too far and meet someone she shouldn't.

"It's early, Amelia. Just have her stay close." Mom said, so I reluctantly let her go with the instructions not to go too far. "You know you're gonna have to face the music at some point."

"Face what music, Mom? He didn't want her. I'm not subjecting my child to that."

"You and I both know that's not Lucas MacArthur. I don't know what's right and what's wrong in this, but I do know that you need to talk to him."

I didn't respond. I wasn't about to start my morning off talking about Lucas, so I got started on prepping our food to cook.

Minutes later, a scream from Riley had me rushing out the door in a panic. She wasn't in plain sight which scared me until I thought to look into the trees a little up ahead.

Sure enough, there was Riley, but she wasn't alone. She stood there, staring at her father as he looked at her.

I rushed to Riley, grabbed her quickly, and turned around to leave.

CHAPTER 4

ucas

"Stop right there. Don't you dare walk away from me." I was so angry right now. I don't know what happened or why, but I knew without a doubt that this little girl was mine. "Amelia?"

She turned around towards me with a look like she wanted to kill me. "I don't have to talk to you or do any damn thing you say, Lucas." Oh, she doesn't, huh? We will see about that.

"Amelia, don't test me. I'm not the same 18-year-old boy you left behind. Don't make me lose myself, not in front of her." I said through gritted teeth.

My eyes looked from her to her daughter...*my* daughter. She was my fucking daughter too. I tried to soften my features so she wouldn't see how angry I was at her mother. "Sweetheart, can you go see your grandmother while I talk to your mommy for a little bit?"

"But I wealy want bweakfast." She looked hesitant.

"Tell ya what. If you let me talk to your mommy, I will make sure you get breakfast from the best place to get a big breakfast on a Saturday morning."

"Umm. Okay, but huwwy, Mista. I hab no patient." She said before walking away, and although I was angry, I couldn't help but to smile at how cute she was with her little sassiness. But as soon as I looked back at Amelia my smile vanished.

"What the fuck, Amelia? What's going on? I have a kid?"

"No." She groaned stubbornly, and it pissed me off.

"Bullshit. She looks just like me. Hell, she didn't even have to say who her mother was because that kid is all me with a splash of you and you know it. What I want to know is why I didn't know about it."

"What the hell do you mean? I told you." She yelled.

"The hell you did. I think I would remember someone telling me I had a fucking kid, Amelia."

"Lucas." She tried to look mad, but her eyes betrayed her when they showed how scared and confused she was, as did her trembling bottom lip. "I texted you and you said she wasn't yours. You didn't want her."

I'm stunned to silence, but only for a moment while I look at her and how vulnerable she looks. I can tell that Amelia isn't the same girl she was five years ago. She's stronger and more fierce, and I assume that came from becoming a mother…but right now, I can see a little bit of the old her. Honest and genuine. What she's saying she believes to be true.

"Amelia, I don't know what text message you're talking about, but I haven't spoken to you since the night of that party." I take a step toward her and she backs up. With every step I took she backed up until she hit the tree. "Why did you leave, Amelia?"

She tried looking away, but I needed to know why so I turned her face back to me. "Because I heard you. You were talking to your friends at the graduation party and...and Bryce said–"

"He said you were a bet." I can never forget that night because I lost one of my best friends, not that I give a shit because he deserved it. "Is that what you heard?"

"Yes." She whispered as a tear rolled down her face. A part of me, the part that still for some reason loved this woman, wanted to reach up and wipe her tears. I wanted to comfort her, but I wouldn't. She left here running, and while I was torn up about it, nothing hurts worse than her not telling me about my kid. I've missed so much.

"And that's why you left? Fuck, Amelia. You could have talked to me. I came over every damn day to try to talk to you. I waited and waited but you never came to me. All this time I have tried to understand why and *this* is the reason? Had you waited just five more damn seconds you would have seen me break his fucking nose and knock one of his teeth out for saying that shit."

My mother had given me shit about my reaction to Bryce. She'd even tried to get us to talk it over, because we never stayed mad at each other...But the more Amelia dodged me, the angrier I got, and reconciling with Bryce was the last thing that I wanted to do.

I paced for a minute before turning back to her. "This is the reason I didn't know about my child? I've protected you my whole life, my whole damn life, Amelia. You knew me better than anyone else. How could you think so little of me? How could you think that I would be capable of hurting you like that? How could you think that I would abandon my own damn child?"

She looked like I had just hit her across the face. She stood there looking at me without saying a word and it only made me angrier. "Amelia, I have no idea what text you're talking about but I'm going to find out. You could have called me, called my mom, hell you could have had yours come down and give me a message. Anything but this."

"Lucas, I tried to–"

"No, Amelia. I have a daughter." My voice broke, and I had to pause and take a deep breath to calm myself. "I have a daughter, Amelia, and she doesn't know me."

Amelia's POV

He's telling the truth. I can see it in his eyes. I've always been able to tell if Lucas was lying. and he isn't, but how can that be?

Listening to him, emotional and hurt by my actions, I don't know what to say. I ran from him and stayed away because I believed what I heard Bryce say and I feel horrible about it. I'm so confused about everything.

"Lucas." I took a step towards him and reached for his hand. I recognized his emotions from all of the years that we spent together, and he was spiraling. I wanted to calm him so we could talk, but he stepped away from me.

"What's her name?" he asked, ignoring the rest of what needed to be addressed.

I hesitated before answering him because I wasn't sure what his reaction would be. "R-Riley." His eyes widened and his shoulders slumped.

"You named her Riley?" His voice was full of emotion. Things were far from fixed, but I do recognize that I played a part in the start of our troubles so I wanted to offer some kind of bridge.

"Yes. I wanted her to have a piece of your family. Her

name is Riley Marie." It was a decision I did not make easily, but regardless of what happened, I wanted her to have something from his family.

I remembered him telling me that he would name his first daughter Riley because it was his baby sister's name. When he was four years old, his parents were pregnant with a baby girl whose name was going to be Riley, but they lost her late in the pregnancy.

"That should make me feel good, but it doesn't." He shakes his head and my heart aches. "I…I'm gonna head home. Well, to my folk's house. Can I come see Riley in a little while?"

"But we need to talk, Lucas."

"And we will, but I'm gonna lose my shit if I don't walk away right now. The last thing I want to do is lash out, especially in front of Riley." He paused for a moment before speaking again. "I'll send my mother over with some breakfast for her."

After that, he turned around and walked away. For a few minutes, I stood there and watched him as he crossed the long path to get back to his house.

Eventually, I walked back to my mother's. As I walked in, I willed myself not to break down in front of my daughter, but my heart and mind had other plans. The moment that I laid eyes on her and could only see a mini Lucas, I lost it. Right there in the corner of the living room, I broke down crying.

I still don't understand the text thing, but I do know that Lucas is telling the truth just like he's telling the truth about graduation night. Which means that this is my fault. Just like my mother said, I should have known better.

"Amelia, you need to calm yourself before you upset Riley." My mom said, and I knew she was right, but I had five years of tears that wanted out. I couldn't be strong any longer.

The tears that I wouldn't allow myself to cry when I was so angry with Lucas.

The tears that I wanted to cry but wouldn't when I was having my daughter alone.

The tears that I wanted to cry when I had sleepless nights, cursing Lucas for not being there with me…I sat there and let it all out.

"Gwandma, I weady to be wiped." Riley yelled from the bathroom. My mom said something and I heard her walk away.

I don't know how long I sat there or how long my mother was gone but suddenly I was enveloped in a tight hug. I knew instantly that it was Marie MacArthur.

"Oh, my sweet girl." She rubbed my hair and kissed the top of my head. It made me cry harder. She should be outraged for her son, but here she is comforting me.

"I'm sorry. He-he's gonna hate m-me."

"Hush now. It's Lucas we're talking about. He could never hate you. He's upset and he's hurting, but he could never hate you." I really hope that's true. "Now, let's get you cleaned up. I don't want our Riley to see you upset."

My mom distracted Riley so I could sneak past her and into the other bathroom. By the time I came out Riley was sitting at the table with the biggest breakfast she's ever had. Of course Mrs.MacArthur still did her big Saturday breakfasts.

"Mommy." Riley squealed with excitement when she noticed me. "Look, Mommy. Gwandma say this is mys other gwandma. Other gwandma say call her Nana and she bwought me bweakfast."

"That's so nice, Ri. Did you say thank you?"

"Uh oh...Thank you, Nana." She smiled with all her teeth at Mrs.MacArthur.

"You're welcome, my darling." Mrs.MacArthur wiped a tear from her eyes. "God, she's so adorable and she looks just like Lucas when he was little."

"Whose Lucas?" Riley asked.

"We-we will talk about Lucas a little later, okay?"

"Okay, Mommy, but member–"

"Yeah, yeah. I know. You don't have any patience."

Before I talk to her about Lucas, I need to actually speak to Lucas. I don't know how he feels or what his plans are. We need to hash everything out and then there are the other complications that I have.

Like the fact that this isn't me and Riley's home. What happens when my mother is feeling better and it's time for us to leave?

CHAPTER 5

ucas

DROWNING...I feel like I'm drowning in my emotions right now and not for the reason that everyone would expect me to be.

Does it hurt that Amelia left town without talking to me or letting me explain and believing the worst of me? Yes, but the most painful part about everything is knowing that she was alone when she went through her whole pregnancy and having Riley. I should have been there.

It must have been a hard time for her. Not only did she have to deal with every single moment of her pregnancy alone, but she had to do it with her heart shattered. I imagine her laying in the hospital, in pain, and no one there to help her, and it fucking guts me. I was supposed to be there. I was supposed to be by her side through it all.

I was robbed of five years of my daughter's life...Amelia's pregnancy, all the doctor's visits and ultrasounds, being there for Amelia when she was sick or needed something, my daughter's birth, her first words, her first steps, and so much more.

Fuck.

"Lucas. Son, let's talk it out." my dad said as he sat on the edge of my childhood bed looking at me as I sat on the floor, leaning against the wall.

By the time I made it to my parents' house I had lost my battle to control my emotions. Since I was coming in from the back, I had to walk through the kitchen to get to my room. My mother noticed me and quickly followed behind me.

I really didn't want to talk about it at the moment. I wanted to talk to Amelia first, but one thing about Marie MacArthur, she doesn't play when it comes to her children. She wouldn't take no for an answer.

Summoning every piece of strength that I could, I told her. "I have a daughter." My voice cracked so bad that it sounded foreign, even to myself.

"You have a what?"

"I have a daughter. I saw Amelia yesterday at the gas station. We didn't talk, because she avoided me and it got to me a little. I went for a walk last night and ended up staying in the old clubhouse. When I woke up this morning, there was a little girl there." I shook my head. I can't believe it.

"Before she could even say who her mother was, I knew that she was mine, Ma, and Amelia had her and never told me."

She had questions…plenty of questions that I wasn't in the mood to answer or more like I didn't have all the answers to them.

With my emotions getting the better of me, I couldn't say much more, but I asked her if she could take Riley some breakfast for me. She left and a few minutes later my father came into the room.

For a moment he sat there quietly letting me wallow in my own pain. My father was always the calm, laid back parent, but when it comes to life and decisions, he was firm.

"Lucas. Up. Now." He said firmly, each word was a strong command. "I understand you're hurting and upset, but you won't hide."

"I'm not hiding. I'm just...I don't know what to do exactly."

"I can't tell you what to do about it, but I know what you're not going to do...blow up on Amelia." I looked at him like he had lost his mind, but before I could say anything he held up his hand.

"You have every right to be upset and hurt, but she raised your daughter alone. Amelia is the most important person to Riley, and my granddaughter is important to me. She doesn't need to see her parents at each other's throats. I won't allow it. Got it?"

"Yeah, Dad. I got it." I said as I nodded my head, but I still couldn't get up and move. I was trying to figure out how I should handle things. She's a little girl. I can't just bulldoze into her life because I want to make up for lost time. And what am I supposed to say when she wants to know why I wasn't there for her?

My dad wasn't trying to be an asshole to me, but he knows his son. My feelings haven't been steady since Amelia left. I went through a lot afterwards and I sometimes lash out when I'm angry, so I completely understand and thank him for his advice.

"Now, Son." He waited for me to look up at him. "It's time to face the music."

. . .

Amelia's POV

A knock at the door has me trembling because I know it's Lucas. I can't move. I'm afraid to face him after he was so upset earlier, so I sit and wait on my mom or Mrs. MacArthur to answer the door.

"You got your head on straight?" I heard her say. I didn't hear a response, but a moment later I heard him walk in. I couldn't face him although I knew that I should.

Silence.

He didn't speak or sit down at first, but I could feel his gaze on me. With a hard sigh he finally sat down on the opposite side of the couch.

"Look at me, Amelia." His voice was soft, but I could hear the indifference in it. He was trying so hard not to show how angry he was. It wasn't working.

Finding the courage, I lifted my head to look at him. I'm expecting him to look angry but he doesn't. He's just sitting there waiting for me to speak but I'm not sure what I should say.

We already determined that the cause of me leaving was a misunderstanding. The text situation isn't solved, but I know that he isn't lying. So, what else do I need to say to help this mess?

"Look…I'm not trying to get into it with you. We need to talk but I would prefer if we did that without Riley or our mothers around if that's okay with you," he said.

"Y-yeah. That sounds good." And I'm glad he suggested it so I will have time to think, because right now my mind is all over the place.

"How do you feel? Are you going to be okay with me getting to know Riley?" What will Riley say when she learns the man that she met this morning is her father? "Amelia, I want to respect you, but now that I know about her, I don't plan on waiting. I want to meet her. Will you be okay with that?"

"Yes. I-I never wanted her to be away from you anyway, Lucas. I just...I believed what I read and I'm sorry for that." Silence. He didn't respond but I could see the hurt in his eyes. He's hurt about not knowing about his daughter, but I think he is hurting more because I believed the worst of him.

Not being able to take the silence, I stand quickly. "I'll get Riley." *Keep it together, Amelia. You have no right to break down and be in your feelings.* "Riley. Come here. I have someone I want you to meet."

"Mommy." She giggles. "Is it Nana? Ise alweady met Nana, silly."

"No, baby, it's not your nana. Just come on." I reached for her hand as we walked back to the living room. Riley paused when she saw Lucas.

"Hi, Mister. Ya feelin betta? You was cwinkly right hea." She pointed to her face. "Mommy say I gets cwinkly when Ise upset like my daddy. Is that how come yous get cwinkly?"

"Umm. I-I don't know. I never paid it any attention really."

"Oh. What's ya name?"

"Lucas." he said, and she gasped.

"Yous Lucas? Nana say I look like Lucas. Yous thank I look like you?" He smiles and laughs a little.

"Dang she sounds just like me when I was a kid." He said to me before turning back to Riley. "Yes, I do think you look like me."

"Why?" She turned her head sideways. Lucas opened his mouth to talk but then looked at me with questioning eyes. I was scared, so fucking scared, but I nodded my head yes.

"Well, sweetheart, I'm your dad." Riley's eyes widened and she whipped them to me really fast.

"But Mommy say...Mommy say Daddy libs weally far. I not thank its far when we came to gwandma's." I didn't know what to say to that. Having a really smart kid is amazing... until it's not. "Why I not see Daddy long time ago?"

"Well, Ri, Mommy made a big mess of things." Her little face scrunched up like she was thinking.

"Like...like when I wasted all the flours when Mommy made cookies?"

"Yeah, baby, but Mommy–" I paused when I felt Lucas's hand on mine. He squeezed my hand gently.

"Riley, come here." When she walked over to him, he sat her down next to him and started talking to her.

"Riley, your mommy...your mommy didn't make a mess, she just made a mistake, okay. Sometimes big people make mistakes but that's okay because she's a good mommy, yeah?"

"Mhm. She plays with me and buys all the snacks. She wead me stowies too."

"Oh wow. That sounds like Mommy is amazing." He rubbed the top of her head. "So you not seeing Daddy doesn't mean that Mommy isn't amazing, it means that Daddy has some making up to do and I promise to never be away from you again. You will see me all the time, okay."

I wanted to cry. He could have left me fumbling to clean up this mess that yes, I made, but he didn't. Lucas would never do that which is another reason for me to feel like crap.

Once again he took care of me...just like he would have back then.

Lucas's POV

. . .

RILEY'S so much like me that it's scary. I could see her little wheels turning in her mind trying to figure everything out and I couldn't leave Amelia out to hang herself.

Technically, I'm a stranger to Riley. Her trust in me can grow, but I didn't want to break her trust in the only consistent thing she's had in her life.

By no means have I forgiven Amelia for the time that I have missed with Riley, but when my little girl looks at her mommy and smiles, I know that I've done the right thing.

When she looks back to me and says, "Okay, Daddy." I almost lost it in that living room, but I held myself together.

Coming over here, I thought for sure Riley would be hesitant to talk to me. I didn't expect her to hold a conversation with me, but here she is talking, smiling, and calling me Daddy for the first time.

"Everything alright in here?" My mom says as she enters the room. I have no idea why she just asked me that. We both know that our mothers were listening to every word we said in that conversation.

"All good, Mom."

"Good, good. Riley, can you go watch your show so I can talk to your Mommy and Daddy for a few minutes?"

"But, Nana…Ise just seen my daddy." I can't help the smile on my face. *My daughter wants* me.

"I'm not going anywhere, sweetheart. After we talk to Nana you can come back, okay."

"Okay, but huwwy. I hab no patient." She groaned a little, making me laugh a little more.

"She's adorable, isn't she?" Mom's eyes were watering for what I'm sure is the umpteenth time today. "Are you taking her over to the house?"

I saw Amelia tense up, but it didn't bother me. If I was her it would make me nervous as well. "I don't know about that, Mom. I was thinking of holding off for a few days."

"Why? Everyone will want to meet her."

"I understand that, Mom, but this is all new to Riley. It's new to me. I don't know how to be a dad, but I know that I don't want to bombard her on the first day. She just met her dad for the first time. Give me a few days."

"And what about Dad? He will want to see his granddaughter."

"And that's fine, but he will have to come here…alone." I don't know a damn thing about being a dad but it seems like a lot to meet your dad and then be forced into a family dynamic all at once.

"Okay. Well, if you insist."

"I do, Mom, and I hope you understand." I knew she did, but I still wanted to make sure. Amelia has always been somewhat shy. I don't want to make this situation more difficult than it already was.

By the end of the day I was emotionally drained. I spent the whole day at Amelia's place with Riley. We watched movies and I ordered lunch.

This was her first day knowing me, so I did it Amelia's way, but that won't always work. I will need to get my place fixed up for Riley and a list of other things.

Today was amazing but now we're at the point where I have to leave, and I hate it. I want to be the one that gives her a bath and tuck her in, but Amelia wasn't ready for that. She didn't say it but the "Riley, it's time to get ready for bed. Tell your daddy goodnight," was a clear indication.

"But I want Daddy to stay. Why can't you stay, Daddy?" Riley said with big tears in her eyes that broke my heart.

"I'm sorry, sweetheart, but I will be right across the yard at Nana's. If you need me, I will be right over."

"Pwomise?"

"I promise. I will see you bright and early, okay."

"Okay." She hugged me tight before letting go and heading for her room.

"Lucas." Amelia said as I walked out the door. She grabbed my hand, and I turned around to face her.

"Yeah? You're not trying to talk about everything this late, are you?"

"No. I just...Lucas, I just...I'm sorry." Her forehead dropped to my chest, something she used to do often, but I couldn't comfort her right now. I just couldn't.

"Goodnight, Amelia." I said as I headed back across the yard.

I'm not surprised when I step into the kitchen and my whole family is waiting for me, siblings included. "What's this about you having a kid? And with Amelia?" my brother Lawson said.

"I just found out myself...by accident actually." I'm still pissed about that.

"And you had no idea?" My sister said.

"Not a clue. Apparently she tried to tell me through text and I supposedly responded saying the baby wasn't mine and that I didn't want her. We all know that I wouldn't say anything like that, especially to Amelia."

"So, who do you think she was texting? Any ideas?" my dad asked.

"Not one, but I know one thing...when I do find out who it is, there won't be a place they can hide. I missed 5 years between Amelia's pregnancy and my daughter's life. Somebody's gonna pay for that."

The more I think about it, the angrier I get, but right now I have other things to worry about...like getting to know my daughter and being the best father to her.

CHAPTER 6

melia

Is it crazy that I wanted him to stay with me? I wanted to put Riley to bed together and sit down and talk, but I couldn't be selfish. I know that I hurt him so I need to give him some time to process that and also time to process that he has a kid.

On one hand, I think anyone could have easily made the same mistake I did. However, on the other hand, *I* should have known better. I know Lucas or the Lucas from 5 years ago. He would have never denied our child, but I was too blinded by what I thought was him hurting me to see the truth.

Now I'm in this weird place of not knowing what to do or how to make it right. It's been 5 years so I can't just go on like nothing has changed between us because it has. We're both different people with different heartaches.

"Mommy, mommy, mommy."

"Yes, Riley."

"Yous not listening, Mommy. Ise weady to get out."

"Sorry, Ri. Mommy was just thinking for a minute. Let's get you out and in bed." Please let her go down easily tonight. I'm so mentally exhausted and could use a drink…or three.

"Ise not weady for bed. I want to see Daddy." Her little round eyes started to water.

"Riley." I pursed my lips to keep from groaning. "Your daddy had to go home. Now if you be a good girl and go to sleep I will get you some ice cream tomorrow and you can share it with your daddy."

Her eyes widened and she moved faster to get ready. For once I was thankful for her obsession with ice cream, something else she got from Lucas. In less than 10 minutes she was asleep.

"Riley in the bed?" my mom asked as I walked into the kitchen. I headed straight for the cabinet where I know she keeps her liquor. I take two shots and a deep breath before looking at her.

"Yep. She's all tucked in. Thankfully it didn't take forever…She wanted to see Lucas again."

"Well, she's excited. She just met her dad so it's normal." While my mother was just speaking facts, I feel like shit when she says things like that.

She made it known before that she didn't think Lucas was capable of what I said he did. So today, finding out that she was right has been a bit irritating to say the least.

"I do understand that, Mom. It's just a little weird for me, ya know? She's known him for less than 24 hours and she's crying for him. I don't know. I guess I didn't expect things to go over so smoothly for the two of them?"

"Is that going to be a problem for you? Are you okay with Lucas being around and it not being for you?"

"I have no choice but to be okay with it. I'm not going to

keep her away from him and you know Lucas...He doesn't forgive easily." He was too damn stubborn for it. When we were kids if he got mad at one of his siblings, he would be mad for weeks and it was over the simplest things. Can't imagine how long he could stay mad over this.

"Well, alright then. Better get some rest. I need you to go to the store for me in the morning to get some things since I wasn't prepared for you."

We said our goodnights and then we headed off to bed. Sleep took forever to come. I laid there for hours thinking about the mess I made and how I could fix it. It felt like I had only just gone to sleep when Riley woke me up for breakfast.

We ate something quick and then left for the store. It was a Sunday so most folks in Forest View were getting ready for morning service. Since Mrs.MacArthur was on call last night, they wouldn't attend, and since my mother usually went with them, she isn't either.

With this being a small town, it's definitely better for me to shop before service. Afterward, everything would be crowded. It also lessens my chances of running into a bunch of people.

"Mommy, how much longer? Gwandma weally gots lots of stuffs." Riley whined.

"Almost done. Then we can get your ice cream."

"Okay, Mommy."

"M-Mommy? Did...She just said mommy." I heard a male voice and turned around. Bryce was standing there holding some roses, eyes wide and skin pale like he had seen a ghost.

"I...umm...L-Lucas doesn't know about her, does he?"

"He didn't. He does now. Why?"

"I'm sorry, Amelia. It's all my fault. I'm the reason he didn't know."

. . .

LUCAS'S POV

REFLECTING on my life over the last five years, I couldn't be happier than I am now. Knowing that I have a daughter and being in her life has been like taking that first breath after drowning. I expected her to be hesitant or to give me shit for not being there, but she hasn't.

I know that she's only four years old, but kids are tough. They don't hold punches or sugarcoat things. Instead, I got a little mini-me that's ready to love me just as hard as I am ready to love her and I am. I have no idea how to be a father, but I'm doing it.

When my phone rings, I'm surprised because no one usually calls me so early on the weekend. When I look down I see that it's Amelia. A smile spreads across my face, thinking that it's my daughter. "Hello."

"L-Lucas."

"Amelia? What's wrong? Why are you crying?"

"Are you at your parents' house?"

"Yes. What's wrong, Amelia?" Dammit, why won't she answer me? "Is something wrong with Riley?"

"No. I will be over in a minute, okay? Just give me a second to set Riley up." She said before ending the call.

I'm pacing back and forth because I can't stand the waiting. A little bit later she knocked at the back door. Her eyes were puffy from crying, and she looked like she would start crying again at any moment.

"Amelia, what's going on?"

"It was Bryce."

"What was Bryce?"

"The text message, the missed calls…it was because of Bryce." Her bottom lip started to tremble.

"What? How do you know that?"

"I saw him at the grocery store. When he saw Riley, he looked shocked. Then he apologized and said that it was his fault you didn't know. God, Lucas...I'm sorry. I'm so sorry, Lucas. I shouldn't have believed it."

"Shh...Come here." I pulled her into my arms. Despite everything, I still can't stand to see her cry.

On the outside, I was calm. I didn't want to upset Amelia more than she was. But on the inside, I was boiling. I wanted to know what the fuck Bryce was thinking and to be honest, I was still mad at her.

"Someone's at the door." My sister Zoe yelled. I continued to hold Amelia. Someone else answered the door.

"Hello. Umm...Is Lucas here?" I froze when I heard Bryce's voice before pulling away from Amelia and rushing out the door.

Bryce's eyes widened when he saw me coming. "L-Lucas." I grabbed a hold of his shirt around his neck.

"Did you have something to do with me not seeing my daughter? Yes or no?" I didn't want to hear anything else that came out of his mouth.

"Yes." That's all he got out before I was knocking him down the steps and following behind him.

"How could you do that to her?" I hit him...one, twice... Hell, maybe even three times before my parents and Amelia started trying to pull me off him.

"Lucas...Stop it." Zoe yelled as she started to cry. "Please stop." She laid on top of him, covering him up to keep me from hitting him. "He's not fighting you back, Lucas. If you hit him again, you will have to hit me first."

Stepping back, I looked at my sister and I don't know how to feel. "You drag your sack of shit out of here before I do it." I groaned as I turned around to go back inside.

"What?" Zoe said confusingly.

"What, you thought I didn't know that you were seeing

him? I knew. I've known the whole time. I just never said anything because it wouldn't matter."

She tried to say something, but I put my hand up to stop her. I'm not interested in anyone's excuses about any of it.

"When it comes to him, your loyalties don't lie with me… They never have." I said before heading up the steps. "If anybody needs me, I will be spending time with my daughter."

CHAPTER 7

melia

"COME ON, AMELIA." Lucas groaned as he walked away.

I hurried behind him, unsure of if he was just upset about Bryce or if I had pissed him off as well. I've never seen Lucas this angry before so I'm in new waters here.

Halfway through the walk I bumped into Lucas when he suddenly stopped and turned around. I wasn't paying much attention because my mind was still a mess from what had just happened.

"I shouldn't have lost my shit like that with you there. I'm sorry for that, Amelia." He looked regretful and ashamed.

"I've seen you get into a fight before, Lucas."

"Yeah, but that was when I was a teenage boy, not the father of your child. I'm glad Riley wasn't there."

"Hey. It's okay. It's understandable how upset you were. Let's just…let's not worry about that right now. Riley has been dying to see you since she woke up this morning."

He didn't say anything else, just nodded his head and started back walking. We didn't speak another word.

A very selfish part of me was wondering what this all meant for Lucas and me. He knows that I didn't mean to keep Riley away from him, and I know now that it wasn't him that I was talking to.

When we were almost to the house the door burst open and Riley came running out. "Daddy," she yelled until she reached him and jumped in his arms.

"Hey, my sweet girl." I swear it's the most amazing thing for them to be like this with each other.

So many times over the years I have imagined what it would be like between them. I didn't expect him to want to fall into the role of being her father so quickly…and I definitely didn't expect her to take to him so well.

Sure, Riley is very outgoing but it's one thing to talk to people comfortably and another to meet your daddy at four years old and pick up like he's been there all alone.

It's a blessing. It could be so much worse, but it's also scary. What if she starts to prefer him over me? What if we can't work out co-parenting?

Those are the things I have thought about since yesterday, and I don't know what to say or do about them.

"Daddy." Riley squeals and laughs while Lucas twirls her around. She's in heaven playing around the yard with him. I can't help but sit back and watch. I feel like I'm intruding but I want to be here.

"Daddy, guess what. I have a puprise for you. Mommy, can you help me give Daddy his puprise?"

"It's too early, Ri. You can give it to him a little bit later." She did her little pout before turning back to Lucas.

"Okay, Mommy. You gonna play with me and Daddy?" I wanted to but when I looked at Lucas and his face was void of any emotions, I decided that it was best to let them have it.

"No, baby. I'm just going to watch you guys." I said to her with the best fake smile that I could give. That's all I did for the rest of the day too. I watched Lucas and Riley have a great day together while I smiled and pretended like it didn't hurt that he didn't want me to join them.

After playing outside, the two of them went inside so Riley could give him his surprise which was basically ice cream and some toppings. It was nothing special, but Lucas reacted like she had given him a million bucks or something.

The two of them filled the room with laughter while watching *Shrek.* They colored and played with toys…they even did her nails.

He stayed all day and night with her. He helped her during dinner and helped her get ready for bed. I was getting ready to tuck her in when he asked if he could. Of course, I said yes, but I didn't want to intrude so I kissed her good night and let her go in with Lucas.

"Daddy."

"Yes, Riley." He spoke softly. Yes, I stood outside the room listening. I couldn't help it.

"Ise just met you." For the first time in her short little life, Riley sounded unsure, and that made me curious about what she wanted to say.

"Yes, sweetheart. Daddy is really sorry about that."

"That's okay, Daddy, but…is it okay that I love you already?"

For a second, he didn't respond and I questioned if I should walk in but then he spoke and his voice was full of emotion. "I love you too, Riley."

A few minutes later, Lucas came out of the room, pausing when he saw me in the hall. "Thank you, Amelia, for letting me spend the day with her. She's…everything. I hate to leave her to be honest, but I have to work in the morning. I'm still going to stay across the way for a few days so if she needs anything, let me know."

Stay. I want you to stay so we can talk. I want you to tell me how I can fix this. Stay. Please. Those were the thoughts that were screaming inside, but instead of saying them, I simply said okay.

"Good night, Amelia. See you tomorrow." Tonight I would let him leave, but tomorrow will be a different story. I've been a bold woman these past five years while I was away. It's time that I start acting like it at home too.

With Riley in bed and the house together, I decide to take a moment for myself. I fixed myself a drink and ran a nice bath. I'm ashamed to say how different fantasies of Lucas were running through my head.

He's always been handsome to me, but watching him love on our daughter and take care of her today has me very hot and horny.

Is it shameful that I found myself leaning back in the tub and touching myself while thinking of him? His name whispered from my mouth every time I brought myself closer to the edge before finally allowing myself to let go.

It has been a very long time since I'd had sex, because being a single mom with trust issues didn't allow time for dating. So, maybe it was a little shameful to touch myself with thoughts of him considering the issues we're facing but, God, did it feel good.

CHAPTER 8

ucas

It's been two days since I've known about my daughter, and I'm starting to wonder how some men don't want to be around their children. I've spent a lot of time with her both days but I'm still not satisfied.

At least I got to tuck her in and read to her today. I would have loved to sleep and wake up with my daughter under the same roof as me, but that will come.

I didn't want to rush and have the conversation with Amelia because I didn't want to do it in an emotional state. When emotions run wild, things are said or taken in a way that they aren't meant and I've got a lot of pent up emotions over this.

This morning is bitter because I won't be able to spend as much time with her but I guess this is something that I will have to get used to. Since Amelia and I aren't together, I can't be with her all the time. I also can't stay at my parents' house forever, but we'll figure it out.

Walking into work, I already know that today is going to be a little more stressful than it normally is. I work for the local bank or more accurately, pretend to work for the bank. My family actually owns the bank and half of the town, but my parents chose to separate us from the day-to-day and I'm thankful for it just like I was when we were growing up.

My mother actually made that choice after growing up in this town herself. She wanted a bit of normalcy. She didn't want the favoritism and everything that came along with it, but it's hard to be normal when your family owns most of the town and the mountains around it.

When I went to school for finance, my parents were excited. A member of our family hadn't actually worked at the bank in a while so they thought it would be a good fit for me. Honestly, I love numbers, I always have, so it was a good fit for me.

"Morning, Mr. MacArthur." my assistant greets me as I walked in.

"Morning, Jenny." I gave her a small smile before walking into my office. Jenny's nice and is very much a wonderful assistant but her best quality is that she hasn't tried to hit on me like some of the other women that I work with.

After Amelia left it took me a while to get the hang of things. Like I said, a part of me thought I had pushed her sexually and it fucked with me mentally. After a while, I casually dated every now and then but never with anyone at work.

I didn't have time for them before but now that my daughter is here, the hell with everyone or everything. I really want to say the hell with work right now too, but I can wait.

"I apologize, Mr. MacArthur. I know you just got in, but

there is a Taylor Mills here that wishes to speak with you. I told her you were busy, but she said she couldn't wait." Jenny winces.

Jenny knows how much I hate starting my day with a meeting. Usually, I like to work with anything that's on my desk first and then move to any appointments and meetings. Not today. Today I figure the faster I get meetings done, the faster I can get home to Riley.

"Send her in, Jenny." Taylor Mills. That's a name I haven't heard in a while. Taylor was a year younger than me, but her older sister Trinity went to school with Lawson. They were really good friends before Trinity sadly lost her life in an accident.

She walks into my office looking every bit of the spitfire she was when we were in school.

Confident.

Head held high.

Determined.

Yep, she means business. "What can I do for you, Taylor?"

"Good morning, Mr. MacArthur. I wanted to speak with you about getting a business loan to open my bakery."

"Taylor, I don't personally deal with loans. We have a department for that. Have you submitted a proposal to them?"

"I have and without even giving me time to explain my plan, they denied me because I don't have enough collateral. I'm here to ask you to consider my proposal. You may not be in the loan department, but you run the bank."

"Hmm." I try my best to stay out of each department's affairs unless I have to. On behalf of Trinity, I will take a look. "Tell you what, Taylor, I will look at everything. Give me a day or two and I will get back to you."

She shakes her head in response. "Something wrong?"

"I sort of need an answer today. I found this perfect

building right on Main street. The owner agreed not to put it on the market for a few days so I could see about a loan. A day or two will be too late."

"I see...Well, alright. I guess I'm taking a look right now." I open the folder that she's prepared and I have to say, she's done a good job. I have no doubt that her business could be successful.

"The good news is I love your plan. You did an excellent job and I know it will be successful long term."

"But?"

"I can't grant you a loan from the bank. From a paperwork standpoint, it won't work." She drops her head and sighs heavily, looking defeated. Now is my time to be more than a wealthy asshole that only cares about the numbers.

"Let me finish, Taylor. When this bank was founded, the family that owned it wanted it to be the type of bank that stood by the small people just as well as the big ones. I believe in your plan, Taylor, so while I can't give you a loan, I'm going to help you."

"How?"

"There's a program that you can sign up for with the bank. It will get you the money you need to start your business and keep it going for a while. There are some conditions like saving a percentage for repairs and things like that, but it will help you get started and stay afloat until your business takes off. The issue is that the processing time is about 7-14 days."

"I'm very thankful. I am, but by then I won't have the building that I've dreamed of. The owners aren't asking much. It won't stay long."

"I understand." I said as I went into my desk. I first handed her the paperwork for the program. Then I signed my name to a check and made it out to her. "Whatever you need to get your building and to get started on repairs before the paperwork is approved.."

Her eyes widened and her mouth dropped as she looked at the check. "This...You're giving me a check? I can't accept this."

"You can. Either you can accept the check or I can go buy the building and gift it to you. Just get what you need, Taylor."

"But...it's your family's name on it. This is a family account."

"And we use it to help people. Now we're helping you."

"Lucas...I mean, Mr. MacArthur. Thank you so much." She said as tears formed in her eyes. "I swear I'm going to pay you back."

"Not necessary. Take what you need and live your dream, Taylor." A few more tears and a couple more thank yous and she was out the door.

The rest of my day was just as busy as my morning. I didn't have time to do anything more than a call with Riley for a few minutes on my lunch break. By the time 4 o'clock arrives, I'm running out the door to make it back to her.

When I pull in, I drive on back to Amelia's house instead of stopping at my parents' house on the way. Before my feet could hit the ground, I heard a squeal from Riley.

"Daddy," she yelled as she ran and jumped into my arms. This is what I've missed out on, my little girl running up to me after a long day. God, I could get used to this.

CHAPTER 9

melia

"MOMMY." Riley gasped. "Ise think that's my daddy." She hopped out of her seat by the window when the car stopped in front of the house. "Daddy" She squeals as she runs up to him.

"Hey, sweetheart...Hey, Amelia." He kissed her on the cheek. Riley's little lip poked out and her eyes welled up. My heart squeezed seeing her like this. She's never had anyone but me so I've never seen her miss someone so much. "Don't cry, Riley. What's wrong?"

"I think she just missed you. She's been in a funky mood all day." I shrugged. "She woke up in a bad mood."

"What's wrong, Riley? You just missed me?" He asked.

"Yeah and…and you not talk to me."

"I talked to you, remember? Daddy was really busy today so I couldn't talk that long."

"You not talk to me last night either when you went to Nana's house but you talked to Mommy."

"Sweetheart, I didn't talk to Mommy after I left. If I did I would have talked to you."

"Uh huh. You did. I heard Mommy when her was in the bathroom and her thought I was sleeping. Yous did and yous didn't want me to know cause her was whispewing."

Oh shit. Please tell me she isn't talking about what I think she is because there was only one time that I whispered his name.

"What?" Lucas's eyebrows were furrowed as he looked from her to me and back again.

"Riley, let's not bother your Daddy, okay? He's here now."

"But I heard you, Mommy. You say 'Lucas. Oh, Lucas." Oh, God, kill me now. "Why you not talk to me too, Daddy?"

There's no telling what Lucas is thinking of me. Sure, I'm not the only woman to touch myself nor am I the first to be heard, but saying his name and pretending that it was him touching when we're not on speaking terms probably makes this shit weird.

I expected him to be pissed off but when I chanced a look at him, he had his mouth balled up to keep from laughing. "Hmm. I think maybe Mommy was excited about the surprise I have for you. Or maybe it was something...else...I said or did that excited Mommy."

"A purprise?" Riley squealed. "What purprise?"

"It's a secret." He whispered. "I have to finish talking to your mommy about it first."

"Okay, Daddy." She beams and just like that she's back to normal. I have no idea what's going to happen when it's time to go home. I took time off work and worked things out with my landlord, but eventually, in a few weeks, I have to return home and so does Riley.

"Lucas." My mom smiled as we walked through the door.

"It's good to see you." Yeah, because seeing him yesterday and the day before that wasn't enough, I guess.

"Good to see you too, Ms. Wallace. I hope you're feeling a little better with Amelia and Riley around."

"Thank you, son. I'm getting there." And thankfully she was. When Mrs. MacArthur called and told me that my mother had been sick, I expected the worst. With us being here she seems to be getting better which leads me to believe a part of it was loneliness.

"So what are we doing today, Riley?" Lucas asked her.

"Ise hab not had my dinner. I waited on you, Daddy. Mommy made baghettis. It's my favowit."

"Is it? Spaghetti is my favorite too." I know it and that's exactly why I made it. Lucas loved spaghetti so much as a kid, one time his mother had to feed him spaghetti for a whole week because he refused to eat anything else.

Throughout dinner, I didn't speak much. I had made up my mind that I was going to talk to Lucas tonight, and I didn't want to give him a reason to leave before I could have my chance.

Once dinner was over I gave Riley a big hug and kissed her cheek. "Ri, I'm going to let your daddy put you to bed while I straighten up the kitchen, okay?"

"Okay, Mommy. Come on, Daddy." She said as she grabbed his hand. I had already planned this earlier today. Him doing bedtime was just to get him out of the kitchen but I knew he wouldn't say no to extra time with her.

By the time he came back in I had the kitchen cleaned and set the table with some wine and mini cheesecake squares. He paused mid-step. "What's this?" he asked.

"It's been a few days. I figured it was about time we talked about everything. Don't you?"

"Yeah. Sure. We can talk." He nodded his head before

coming to the table and taking a seat. "I wanted to talk to you anyway about Riley."

"Oh. Okay. What about Riley?"

"You know I don't live on the property anymore. I live closer to my job. I know I just met her, but I would like to be able to take her to my place to spend some time with her... have her a room set up and everything."

Well, that wasn't what I was expecting nor was I expecting the reaction that I had on the inside. I keep telling myself that I wouldn't reject this, that I could be okay with him taking her back to his place, but a part of me is afraid to let this change happen. The reality is that I'm not Riley's only parent anymore, and it's something that I will have to get used to.

Lucas's POV

Amelia tried to hide her reaction, but I saw it. I can tell that she isn't quite ready for me to take Riley away to my place. The rational part of me understands. I've known my daughter for less than a week, so her thoughts aren't unreasonable.

Try telling that to the irrational part of me. The part of me that feels like he's missed too much of his daughter's life to waste another second. That part of me wants to make up for lost time.

That part of me wants to demand my time without thinking about anyone else's feelings, but I know that it's wrong. Being an asshole would only hurt my daughter and that's not what I want.

I want to spend my off days spoiling my daughter,

cooking for her, watching movies, reading, or just spending a lazy day in. I just want to be her dad.

"Oh...I...well, of course I want her to spend time with you." She said hesitantly.

"But?"

"It's not necessarily a but. I guess it's something that I will have to get used to. I've never slept away from her."

"Yeah. I understand that and if you need to for the first time you can come with her, but I've been an absent father for her entire life. I don't want to waste another minute." Her face twisted in pain. I wasn't trying to throw any of it in her face. I was only trying to plead a case to spend time with Riley.

"And I'm sorry about that, Lucas. I really am and that's something else that I wanted to talk to you about." She paused as she looked down and fidgeted with her hands. "How long will you hate me for this?"

"I don't hate you, Amelia. I'm hurt and disappointed that you would think that I could hurt you and my child like that, but I don't hate you. I could never hate you." And that was the truth. I can't say that I can go back to the way we were with the snap of my fingers, but I don't hate her.

"Well, it feels like it. I've never felt so distant from you since the day we met, not even when I was away. I feel like you and Riley are living and I'm just watching. I know that you will need some time alone with her, but it just hurts. I know I have no right to feel that way or to rush you."

"I just need some time to adjust, Amelia." She nodded her head, but it looked like that was the last thing she wanted to do. I'm not trying to be an asshole. I just need some time to process the last five years and this sudden change and I'm not going to let her guilt trip me about it.

The problem is, Amelia isn't used to me being upset with her. She's used to me just giving in and forgiving her at the push of a button, but this is different and despite what anyone may say, my feelings are valid.

"I'm taking off on Friday. I would like it if Riley could stay at my place on Thursday and then Friday, since I usually stay at my parent's place, she can meet everyone then. If you need to, you're welcome to come with her, Amelia, but please give me this time with her."

"Okay. I...I will let her go. I don't have to be with her. I trust you, Lucas." She said as she looked into my eyes. Not wanting to say something I didn't mean or that I wasn't sure of, I only nodded my head. A few minutes later I said my goodbyes and walked out the door.

The ride home was...peaceful. I rode in silence, giving myself the time to think about everything that's happened and how I want to handle things. I was almost to my place when my phone rang with my brother's annoying ass ringtone that he set on my phone one day.

"Yo." I answered.

"Don't yo me like we're cool when I haven't even met my niece yet."

"Dude, I told you I would bring her around after she was comfortable. You will meet her on Friday. Until then, don't call my phone with that shit."

"It was just a joke, Lucas. I understood where you were coming from about the whole thing. What's got you so damn grouchy?"

"My bad, Law. It's just been a long day. I'm just leaving Amelia's place seeing Riley and then she wanted to talk."

"Well, have you forgiven her already? We both know that you will because you're still in love with her." I was and every time I thought about everything, I felt stupid for it. I went through hell after Amelia left and as hard as I tried to, I never fell out of love with her.

"It's not that easy. I just...She–"

"She hurt you and she didn't trust you. I saw how destroyed you were after she left so I understand, but she was an 18 year old kid, Lucas. I'm sure she was afraid and confused at the time. Think about it."

"I will, Lawson. I'm pulling up at home so I will talk to you later." I said before ending the call. Logically, I knew Lawson was right. I needed to find it within myself to forgive Amelia.

I can't say that I could see myself getting back with her, but I do need to work towards forgiveness. If I don't do it for anything else I need to do it for Riley.

Walking into my house, I headed straight for my guestroom. Currently, it only has a bed and a desk. I have a lot of work to do in here before Riley comes over.

On the inside, I'm nervous as hell. Giving her a pretty room full of stuff won't mean shit. She's only been with her mom since she's been born. What will she think about coming to stay the night with me? WIll she even want to come with me?

I was uncertain about a lot of stuff, but I was sure about one thing...I will do whatever it takes to be in my daughter's life.

CHAPTER 10

melia

THE LAST FEW days have been…pleasant. That's the only word that I can use to describe them. I wish that I could say that they were amazing, but they weren't. They also weren't horrible. Which leaves me with just, pleasant.

Lucas came over every evening as promised to see Riley. While I still didn't feel welcomed into their growing bond, he was more relaxed around me. He didn't tense up every time I spoke to him about something which sadly is progress.

Honestly, it's not surprising how he's acting. I may be upset about it but it's just because Lucas has never been this way with me, but this is how he is with every other person. It takes him forever to forgive someone and that's if he decides to forgive them at all.

He doesn't do it to be an asshole, but he expects what he gives. He's always been a great friend and he's crazy loyal which was why I was so shocked when I heard the conversation between him and Bryce five years ago.

As I have had time to reflect on what happened over the past few days, I realized that me running had more to do with my own fears and insecurities than anything else. Five years ago, I was genuinely confused why Lucas would want me.

I was nerdy, awkward, and not to mention struggling financially. He was the complete opposite. He was…everything and he wanted me. So when I heard them talking that night I thought it was a confirmation of my fears…that he didn't really want me at all, but I was wrong.

"What are you in here thinking so hard about?" My mother asked as she came into the kitchen. I'm thankful for her interrupting my thoughts before I slide down a rabbit hole of misery.

"Just thinking in general. Taking a moment while Riley naps. I don't want her to be tired when Lucas gets here so I had her lie down for a while." The small smile I gave betrayed how I felt on the inside.

"Today's the big day, huh?"

"It is." I said bitterly before taking another sip of the tea I had been drinking to try and calm my nerves.

"Are you going to be okay?"

"Do I have a choice?"

"Yes. You always have a choice." She reached over, grabbed my hand, and gave it a little squeeze. "Be patient with him, Amelia. He went through quite a bit of self-destructive phase when you left. When his thoughts and feelings catch up, you two will be just fine."

"Mom, why didn't you ever say anything about what Lucas was going through?" That I don't understand. She keeps saying he went through stuff, but she never says what actually happened after I left.

"Well, I tried reasoning with you that there must be more to the story. You were firm on your belief that you were correct. You were heartbroken and sad. I wasn't going to upset you anymore than you already were."

"Mmm." I hummed. I mean, what else could I say. She's right. At the time I didn't entertain the idea that I could be wrong. When she tried to talk about Lucas I refused to listen.

"Anyway…get you some rest today and have a moment for yourself. You will miss her. It won't be easy mentally, but you haven't had a break since you had Riley. You deserve that too."

"I know, Mom. Thank you."

The rest of the afternoon flew by and all too soon I could see Lucas's car coming down the long driveway. "Oh, Mommy. That's my daddy." Riley yelled and jumped up and down. "My daddy's hea."

As soon as the car stopped she was at the door opening it. "Hi, Daddy. Yous coming to get me?"

"Hey, Ri. I am. Are you ready to have some fun with Daddy?...Hi, Amelia." He said after Riley hummed her response.

"Hey. Let me get her bag and her car seat."

"Thanks, but that's okay. I picked up a car seat and me and her are going to do some shopping. Unless she has a favorite toy or blanket, we're good."

"Oh. Okay. Well, she doesn't have one so–" *Be happy that he's prepared, not sad that you're not needed.* I had to say that to myself over and over.

"Well, I guess we better get going then. I will have her back tomorrow evening…Riley, tell your mommy bye."

"Bye, Mommy."

"Bye, baby. Be good for your daddy." I watched him strap her into her new car seat. I watched him climb into the driver's seat, he started his car and pull away. I stood there and watched them until I could no longer see his car or the dust from his tires.

Great. Now what do I do? *You could always stalk them on social media.*

LUCAS'S POV

"DADDY, YOUS DWIVING WEALLY SLOW." Riley groaned for the umpteenth time since we left her mother's house about 20 minutes ago. "Go fastew, Daddy."

"This is fast enough, Riley. I told you I have precious cargo in here."

"What's pwecious ca….ummm. What ya say, Daddy?"

"Precious cargo and you're the precious cargo."

"Ise not, Daddy. Yous silly. Ise Riley." She cracks me up. Man, how I wish that I could have seen her when she was just learning to talk and as a terrible two year old. I wonder if it was just as cute then. She probably drove Amelia crazy.

"Okay. I guess I will go a little faster." Okay so I was being super safe. First of all I have never driven a kid around that was this small. My younger siblings didn't ride with me when they were four years old. And this is my first time driving my own daughter. Safety comes first.

Minutes later we pulled up to the mall. Our mall isn't huge like the bigger cities, but it will do for what we need to get done. Our first stop was *Target.* I had set up the bed and dresser that I rushed out and bought Riley, but other than that the room was bare.

"Okay, Riley, we need to get some stuff for your room. We need some sheets and covers, some curtains, and whatever else you want. What should we get on them? What ya like?"

"Hmm." She hummed as she put her little index finger to the tip of her mouth. "Umm, I think I likes wainbows, Daddy. Can we get some wainbows?"

"Rainbows it is. Don't let go of my hand, okay." I may seem calm but on the inside I was terrified that I would fuck this up some kind of way and Amelia would never trust me with her again.

"This way, Daddy. Come on."

Somebody should have told me that it was not a good idea to take a little girl to *Target* to get her room started. I told myself that we would get her linens, some decor, a few outfits, and just a couple toys and some books.

I didn't want to over do it but my God, it's hard to tell my little girl no. If Amelia saw all the shit in my buggies she would probably be pissed but Riley did that little lip thing and gave me crocodile tears…I was through.

The only time that didn't work was when she wanted this giant teddy bear. It was so big and I already felt like she had enough toys so I told her no. Then she hit me with the "pwetty pwease, daddy." The damn bear is so big I had to put him in the front seat and strap him in like he was a passenger.

"Daddy, can we go to the place so I can get beawy a fwiend?" Riley asked as we're now on the way home to put this stuff away…or at least that's what we are supposed to be doing.

"What place, Riley?"

"Yous know, Daddy. The peoples gets all the white stuff and put it in the little beawy and then yous buy him clothes." Oh hell.

"Are you talking about Build a Bear?" Please say no.

"Yes. That's it, Daddy. We going to that place cause the peoples nice." I think she thinks I'm a fool or maybe just hers because I damn sure want to say yes but…

"I think maybe we need to ask Mommy first. We don't want to get in trouble, okay? We will call her when we get home."

"Okay, Daddy, and Ise need a snack. My tummy is empty. Yous said we would get one. Ise told ya I hab no patient, daddy. Now mys patient weally bad." I shouldn't laugh at her sassiness, but it's so adorable.

"I did give you a snack and then we both said you would get some cookies and milk when we got home, remember?"

"Ise member yous giving me some apples. Apples not a snack, Daddy, that fwuits. Yous silly." I'm starting to think that when she says I'm silly that she really wants to say stupid.

"My mistake. We will be home in two minutes." I looked in the rearview mirror and caught her giving me a slight nod with her lips pursed like she wanted to say more.

We pulled up shortly after. We headed in to grab her snack before going back out to grab everything. Once she was done with her cookies and milk, she let out a huge sigh like she was finally satisfied after years of starvation.

Four trips to the car later and we are now standing in her room looking at a pile of stuff. Well, I'm standing. Riley has propped her little shopping butt in her little chair that's by her bed with her feet up.

"Well, let's get started with putting your things away and then we have to figure out what we're going to do for dinner."

"Can we call Mommy? I hab a queshin." This child. Pulling out my phone, I called Amelia and she picked up so fast you would think she was sitting there holding the phone.

"Lucas? Something wrong? Is Riley okay?" She rushed everything out in a jungle of words. Maybe she *was* holding the phone waiting for me to call.

"Everything's fine, Amelia. Riley wanted to ask you something." She took a breath full of relief. I'm going to try not to be offended or assume she thought I had already fucked up.

"Oh. Okay. Where is she?" I went and sat down on the bed and pulled her in my lap.

"Hi, Mommy?" She waved and gave the biggest smile. That's when I knew the child was about to try and con her mother.

"Hi, Riley. Everything okay?"

"Yes. Me and Daddy got lots of stuffs for my woom. I wanted to go to…what's it called, Daddy?"

"Build a Bear."

"Yes, that. I wanted to go but Daddy say he habs to ask you so he won't gets in twouble."

"Why would you get in trouble for that, Lucas?" Her eyebrows furrowed.

"Well…I don't think you're going to be too happy with me after you see her room." She cocked her head to the side.

"Let me see." I winced before turning the camera around and showing her and she gasped.

"Lucas."

"I know. I know, Amelia. We went to *Target.*"

"You have to put her on a limit. You can always say no or later."

"I tried, but then she said 'pwetty pwease' and I was done." Instead of her being mad she actually laughed like it was the funniest thing.

"Welcome to my world. Jeez, you're going to be forever getting that together." She's right and I still have to figure out dinner and then, do bath and bedtime. Maybe I should have gotten her room together first before picking her up. I just thought it was a good idea to let her pick out her stuff.

"Well…would you like some help?"

I know an olive branch when I see it. I could continue to be a stubborn ass but two things were true. One is that I did in fact need some help and the other is that I recognize that she's trying to make amends.

Maybe I should let her.

CHAPTER 11

melia

YES, I was sitting there with my phone waiting for a call. It had nothing to do with me not thinking that Lucas was capable of taking care of our daughter. It had more to do with the fact that I had never been away from her.

So when he called and nothing was wrong, I was relieved that it was just Riley being her usual self. I couldn't help but laugh at all the stuff he bought for her room. Normally I wouldn't allow Riley to have so many toys from one trip, but I knew that he was just excited to have her, and I wouldn't rob him of that feeling.

When I saw how he looked a little overwhelmed with everything that he needed to do, I saw an opportunity and took it. Nothing has worked so far, and I thought it wouldn't work this time but…

"Umm…Actually, that would be nice," he said, and it took

every bit of self control not to scream with excitement. "I hate to bother you on your first break though. Are you sure?"

"It wouldn't be a bother at all." Please don't change your mind.

"Well, if you're sure, I will text you my address. We will try to be as quick as possible so you can enjoy the rest of your break."

"Alright. I will be right over." I said before hanging up. I went to my room and grabbed my bag and shoes.

"Where are you headed?" My mom asked.

"To Lucas's house to help him with Riley's stuff. He went a little crazy in the store. I'm just going to help him set up."

"Alright then. Drive safe."

I knew that Lucas hadn't had time to stop for dinner so I stopped and grabbed the three of us some sandwiches, salads, and pasta from the diner downtown.

It only took me a few minutes to get to his house from there. He lived right outside our little downtown area. Some nice townhomes had been built here since the last time I lived here. They were beautiful.

Before leaving the car, I took a moment to gather myself. I *needed* to remember that I was here to help Lucas and to get us to a point that he could be cordial with me because we needed to co-parent. I was not here to get things started back between us. Priorities. I needed to remember this and so did my stupid heart that desperately wanted him back.

Grabbing the food, I headed to the door and rang the doorbell. "Coming." Lucas yelled from somewhere in the house. When he opened the door, I had to bite my lip to keep from laughing. His hair was a mess from running his hand through it over and over.

"Hi."

"Hi." For a moment we stared at each other until Riley broke the spell.

"Mommy." She ran up and hugged my legs tightly. It really did my heart some good, because when Lucas is around, I'm basically nothing. It felt good to know that she missed me.

"Hello, Ri. Have you been a good girl for your daddy?"

"Yes. Daddy's not been good though." I looked at Lucas and he shrugged his shoulders.

"Oh really. What did Daddy do?"

"Ise don't know, Mommy, but him say he gonna be in twouble when you gets hea." She said before running off.

"How bad is it?"

"Well, I will let you see for yourself. Thanks for bringing dinner." He took the bags and put them in the dining room before leading me to what I assume is Riley's new room.

"Oh, wow. Lucas, what in the world?" It was a disaster. He showed me the pile of bags earlier but it didn't do this mess any justice. He had tried sorting everything out, but I think that was the wrong thing to do because the floor was covered.

"I know. There's more in the closet too." He sounded a little embarrassed.

"Well, how about you fix Riley's plate and I will get started in here. Is there a certain way you want her room set up?"

"No. Anything you help with is fine...Thank you, Amelia." He said before grabbing Riley's hand and walking out the door.

First things first, we need to get these clothes hung up. Sounds easy enough until I opened the closet and saw that it was half full already. Oh, boy. Thankfully he had a dresser so I got started on folding her pajamas, socks, and underwear.

A few minutes later I was consciously aware that Lucas was standing at the door. He didn't say anything or move for a few minutes. Then, he came and sat down on the floor near me but not next to me and started to help fold.

We didn't talk but that was okay. We were in the same space and there was no tension in the air. That was enough for me…for now.

It had been a little while when Lucas got up and said that he was going to check on Riley. He came back minutes later saying he had set her up with a movie so we could finish some things, but there's no way we would be done with everything tonight.

After about an hour more we had managed to put away all of her clothes, rearrange her toys in a tote, and set up her bookshelf. "Okay, what else are we doing tonight?" I asked him.

"I'm just going to hang this picture so she can have something on her wall. I will put the rest of her things up later and set up her bathroom."

He got a nail and hung the picture while I picked up the trash. When we were done I did a full turn to check everything out. "We made some really good progress." I said.

Lucas looked at me and cocked his head to the side and looked into my eyes. "Yeah, we sure did." The way he looked at me it felt like a double meaning…or at least I hoped it did.

CHAPTER 12

ucas

HAVING Amelia over turned out not to be so bad. Not that I was expecting it to be, but I wasn't sure how comfortable things would be. It was...nice. We got to do Riley's room together, and it felt intimate in a way.

Both of us were sitting down on the floor preparing things for our daughter. My chest filled with a feeling that I didn't expect...yearning. For a few moments I got lost in my thoughts of what ifs. If things had happened differently, would the three of us be a family right now?

Those thoughts continued in my mind until I eventually forced myself to focus on something else. Regardless, I enjoyed the time with Amelia tonight. We didn't talk much but when we did it felt light. I can tell it made her happy too.

"Thanks for helping me with everything. I appreciate it."

"No problem." She stood awkwardly like she was trying to figure out what to do next.

"I'm going to get Riley in the bath. You sit down and eat." I said. We headed out, her to the kitchen and me to the living room to get Riley. She was half asleep by the time I made it to her.

"Daddy, yous took too long. Ise sleepy now." She reached up for me.

"Sorry, Riley, but that's what happens when you try to buy everything in the store. Come on. Let's go tell Mommy goodnight so you can take a quick bath."

When we made it to Amelia, she reached for her and hugged her tight. "Can't yous stay too, Mommy?" Amelia's eyes went wide.

"Oh no, baby. Mommy can't stay. I don't have a room here. Just you and Daddy."

"But mommies and daddies hab the same woom. Yous can sleep with Daddy." Amelia choked on what had to be nothing but air because she wasn't eating or drinking anything at the moment.

"Riley…Not all mommies and daddies live together. You know this, right? It's just been me and you living together, not Daddy."

"But yous could. Yous can stay. Pwetty pwease." Well, shit. She'd gone and pulled out the 'pwetty pwease' on me, and I can't say no to that.

"Don't worry, sweetheart. Mommy's staying." I said. Then, I grabbed Riley and walked toward her bedroom, leaving Amelia standing there looking like she had seen a ghost.

A quick bath and a story later and Riley was off to bed. I tucked her in with one of her new bears, set her night lamp up, and cracked the door.

When I walked back out to the dining room Amelia was still sitting at the table. She had barely touched her food and when she saw me entering her eyes shot up. She looked nervous.

"Why haven't you eaten, Amelia?"

"Lucas, I don't have to stay. I don't want to intrude and make you uncomfortable." She said softly.

"I'm not uncomfortable. What would make me uncomfortable is lying to my daughter. You can take my bed and I will sleep on the couch. It's no biggie."

"I can take the couch."

"Not happening. Now, let's eat and I will get you something to put on." She slightly nodded her head and started back eating. We ate dinner without saying a word. I was trying so hard not to be tense and short with her but the truth is, as much as I felt like this was right, my mind was still cloudy from everything.

"All done?" I asked, because she was just sitting there moving her fork back and forth on a few pieces of salad. She nodded her head slowly. "Come on. Let me get you all set up."

I rummaged through my drawers and grabbed her some of my boxers and a shirt. Pulling her into the bathroom because she was just standing there, I got everything she needed for her shower and was about to head out but stopped with a heavy sigh.

"What's wrong, Amelia?" She looked at me for a moment, opening her mouth and then closing it.

"I'm sorry."

"I know. Let's not talk about this tonight."

"I don't mean that."

"Well, what do you mean? What are you sorry for?"

"I'm trying not to–." She shook her head. "Nevermind."

"You're trying not to do what?"

One second she was staring at me and the next second her lips were on mine.

. . .

Amelia's POV

I tried not to make a move on Lucas. I told myself that I would not touch him first. I would respect his space but being in his bedroom and now his bathroom, such a small space, with him made me feel things. At that moment I wanted him more than anything.

Not that I wasn't already feeling hot and horny. Watching Lucas being a doting father to our daughter made me hotter than watching porn.

Lucas would never make his move on me right now. I know this. I wanted to be more of the bold Amelia that I was when away. I wanted him without a shadow of a doubt and judging by the way he's pulling me closer, he wants me to.

I made the first move by kissing him, but it's him that deepens the kiss. It's him that's stripping my clothes away and lifting me on the counter. "Fuck." He groans before sucking a nipple into his mouth. I can't help the moan that comes from me. It feels so good.

Other than a few toys, I hadn't been touched since the first time that we were together. Not that I was saving myself for anything but as a single mom, afraid to leave her baby, that left me no room for dating. So, my body's sensitive right now, especially to his touch.

He takes his time as he sucks on one nipple and rubs the other, switching back and forth. Sadly, I could probably come like this, but it wouldn't be enough to satisfy me right now. I needed his dick.

"Lucas…Please." I begged. I don't know how long it had been for him but for me, I was desperate. Fourplay or anything else can come later. Right now, I needed to be fucked.

Lucas rushed to his bedroom while undressing at the same time. He came back with a condom. I groaned at the sight of his dick, standing fully erect, looking like it needed me just as much as I desperately needed it.

He chuckled when he heard me. "Like what you see?" He said as he rolled the condom on with one hand while his other hand rubbed my clit. "Fuck, you're wet."

He wasted no time. He lined himself up with my entrance and entered me slowly as his lips found mine again. He tortured me slowly with every thrust and just when I was getting used to him again, he slammed into me...harder and harder.

"Amelia...You feel so fucking good." He moaned as he thrust into me. I couldn't speak. The only sounds that were coming from me were soft cries and heavy panting. "You're going to come. I can feel you...Come for me, Amelia."

I did. I came just as he demanded. "God, Lucas...Oh my God." I moaned, finally finding my voice.

"Aaahhh...Fuck. Mmm." Lucas moaned as he came with me. He pushed into me a few more times before coming to a stop. We still couldn't get enough of each other so without moving we kissed. His tongue slid into my mouth...It felt so good but then suddenly he stopped.

After catching his breath, he straightened up and looked at me for a moment. I knew then that the fog had been broken. Whatever he was feeling was gone now.

"I...I will shower in the other bathroom." He said before walking away. He paused at the door, turned around and looked at me. He was conflicted, I could see that. It was written all over his face. He wasn't sure how he felt about what just happened or if he should stay or go.

I desperately wanted him to stay but as good as the sex was, I'm not naive to think that he's suddenly mine again.

When he closed the door, I started the shower and got in. I wouldn't feel sad over this because I got what I wanted, just not everything. He gave me his body, but I still couldn't have him.

My time in the shower was spent reflecting over the day. It was a good day but one that could make tomorrow awkward.

That was a thought that brought up many questions for me and even as I lay in bed my mind is full of them but only one question matters tonight...How can I win Lucas's heart again?

CHAPTER 13

ucas

WHAT WAS I THINKING? I could see how Amelia was looking and a part of me knew that she was hoping things would move forward with us, but I wasn't ready, and I didn't want to give her false hope.

I had every intention of turning her down if things advanced but when her lips connected with mine, I lost it. All I wanted in that moment was to feel what I felt with her all those years ago.

I would be lying if I said it wasn't amazing because it was. It was better than anything that I had ever experienced, and I couldn't get enough...until it was over and the guilt came crashing down.

If I was going to be with Amelia, it would have had to be all in. I can't casually sleep with the mother of my child without it hurting my daughter, so I was pissed, not at her but at myself.

I have to do better because we will be in each other's lives for a long time. Co-parenting can't work if she thinks all I'm trying to do is get my dick wet.

I damn near ran out of that room last night. I didn't sleep much after showering and coming to the living room. My mind stayed on Amelia all night. My mind once again wandered to thoughts of me taking advantage of her. Sure, she came onto me, but I could have stopped it. I could have said no.

Get your head in the game, Lucas. You don't have time for this shit. Your only focus is your daughter and getting to know her.

I was exhausted as hell, but based on what Amelia told me, I knew my ball of energy having daughter would be awake in no time.

I wanted her first time staying over to be great. I didn't want to give her any reason to want to stay away. Gathering the little strength I had, I reluctantly got up, dropped a pod in the coffee machine and got started on breakfast.

I took out my ingredients and mixed up the pancake mix. I was just about to turn the griddle on when I heard Amelia clear her throat. "Morning." She said as she walked over towards me. My stupid ass brain instantly fogged seeing her in my clothes. "Lucas?"

"Sorry. Good morning. I was just fixing some breakfast so it's ready when Riley gets up."

"Want some help?" She sounded hopeful and maybe I should accept her offer but my body didn't need to be close to hers.

"I've got it. You can just grab some coffee and relax." I started cooking the breakfast and just when I was finishing Riley came into the kitchen dragging one of her bears by the ear.

"Morning, Daddy…Ise weally hungwy today." She said with a yawn.

"Good morning, Riley and you're always hungry." I chuckled as I lifted her up on the stool.

"Mommy say Ise a gwowing girl. Ise need my food… Where is Mommy, Daddy?"

"Umm…I think she went to get changed." I hand her a plate of food. "You go ahead and eat because we have a long day ahead of us. Lots of people want to meet you."

"Mhm. I gets to meet Gwampa." She's excited to meet my dad for some reason. She didn't care much that she would meet other kids. When I told her about them, she didn't blink an eye but the moment I told her about my dad she was ready to go.

"Stay right here and eat, Riley. Let me go and check on your mommy." It had been a while since Amelia left, and I knew Riley would be up looking for her at any moment. I was about to walk into my bedroom when I saw her through the door.

She was sitting on my bed staring ahead. I guess she felt my presence because she slowly turned her head toward me. "Everything okay?" I asked her.

She swallowed hard, and her eyes looked sad before she quickly changed her features. "Yeah. Everything's fine. Is Riley up?"

"Yeah, she's up and eating."

"Okay. I will be in there in a minute to tell her bye and then I will head home. You and Riley have a long day ahead of you, and I don't want to be in the way." I never said she had to go or that she was in the way so where the hell did that come from.

"Amelia…Is everything okay? Something wrong?" I was quite sure that I hadn't done a damn thing since I was just in the kitchen cooking for our daughter, but something in her look told me I did.

"No, Lucas. Nothing's wrong."

. . .

Amelia's POV

Everything was wrong. What did I expect this morning from Lucas? Hell, I didn't know but it wasn't the coldness that I got. Well, maybe not cold...He wasn't cold, just dismissive.

I wasn't a fool to think that having sex would fix everything, but I was hoping that we could have some kind of conversation about what happened last night. Hell, from the way that he was acting, it was like last night meant nothing to him, and I refused to believe that.

Earlier when I offered to help him with breakfast, it was more about seeing if I could talk to him while we waited for Riley to wake up. When he refused my help, I just went back to the room to think of ways to earn his trust again.

Look, I know I was a coward in some ways. A better woman would have put big girl pants on and came out and said what she wanted but not me. I was too afraid of him rejecting me. I was also afraid that pushing him would only make him want distance.

I took a moment before coming out into the kitchen where Riley and Lucas were sitting down eating. "Morning, Ri," I said as I walked up and kissed her forehead.

"Morning, Mommy." She smiled with a mouth full of food.

"Well, I'm going to head home. I will see you and your daddy later on, okay?"

"You didn't want any breakfast?" Lucas asked.

"Oh no, thank you. I've already hijacked your time long enough." Lucas sighed heavily and mumbled something that I didn't understand before turning to face me completely.

"Amelia." He said firmly. "Stay. Sit. Eat." He gestured with his hand towards a plate that he had apparently fixed for me. I nodded my head and whispered a thanks before sitting down and eating with them.

As I sat and enjoyed breakfast with my daughter and her dad, I realize that I've been going about this all wrong. I've just been worrying about how I can get Lucas to forgive me or how I can win Lucas over but that's not what I should be focusing on.

I should be focused on building a working co-parenting relationship and supporting Lucas when it comes to Riley. Eventually doors will open for us to have a talk about everything else. Until then, I will be patient.

"Thanks for breakfast. I'm heading home. I will see you guys later." I said after we were done. I hugged Riley and walked towards the door. Lucas came up behind me and reached for the doorknob before I could.

"See you later...Are you coming to my parents' house when she meets everyone?" He asked.

"I would like to if you don't mind."

"I don't mind at all. We should be leaving here in a few hours. I will text you when we're on the way."

"Alright." I walked down the steps and got into my car. I took a long and deep breath before pulling away. Regardless of what happened, I felt good about the progress that we made yesterday when it comes to working together for our daughter.

When I got home I honestly climbed right back into bed. I did sleep the night before, but I dreamed all night about Lucas and what we had done. I needed a little sleep before going over to see the many MacArthurs.

A few hours later I am awakened by my phone notifications. Lucas and Riley were headed to his parents' place. I quickly got up, took a very quick shower, and threw on some clothes.

I was surprised, but I could see that I beat them there once I had walked across the path. Zoe was standing out back on the phone, but she quickly ended her call when she saw me walk up. "Amelia." She smiled. "How have you been?"

I was shocked by her greeting. She was always nice to me and we got along quite well but considering the shit show the other day and what happened between me and her brother, I didn't expect her to be so friendly. "I've been well, Zoe. How are you?"

"I've been great. Well, maybe not great. I've been good except for my brother's outburst the other day."

"Well, no offense, but what did you expect from him finding out that Bryce was the reason he didn't know about Riley." Why can't I be this bold when I'm talking to Lucas?

"I understand and as much as I would like to plead Bryce's case, I know better. He's not trying to dismiss his guilt or anything...You know what...forget about the whole Bryce thing. Seriously, I'm just ready to meet my niece. I've heard so much about her...I bet Lucas has been hovering all over her."

"He has, but it's sweet. He doesn't want to miss a thing with her and I love it."

"And what about you and Lucas?"

"What do you mean?"

"Are the two of you going to reconcile?"

"I have no idea. You know this was a big deal for Lucas, for all of us really. I don't want to rush anything. I have tried to make advances but he's holding back. I'm going to have to be patient with him." I shrugged.

"Or you can always go for what you want. Look, I know that you would never purposely hurt my brother even if I didn't know what Bryce did. You two were always meant to be, everyone saw it but you guys. He still loves you, Amelia."

I shook my head. "I don't think so, Zoe. I can't see it. He doesn't even treat me like there is a possibility of us reconciling."

"You know how Lucas is. He probably thinks he's doing the right thing by respecting you as the mother of his child. The only time that you've had together has been when the two of you were co-parenting around Riley. You have to get him outside of being a dad and show him that you're not just the mother of his child but also a woman."

"What the hell does that even mean, Zoe?" She smiles evilly.

"It means that the MacArthurs are going out tonight, and you're coming with us."

Oh, hell.

CHAPTER 14

ucas

AFTER AMELIA LEFT, Riley and I got dressed and then we headed back to the mall to go to Build A Bear. Call me a pushover because there's no way that I can say no to my little girl. Two hours and a whole lot of money later, we are heading to my parents' house.

I had no idea one child could spend so much money in one place. I lost count of the amount of times she looked at me like I was a dumbass and said, "But, Daddy. The beawies habs to hab clothes." It's a freaking teddy bear. How many outfits does it need?

"How long, Daddy?" Riley asked.

"About 2 minutes. Nana lives just through those trees up ahead."

"Okay, cause Ise hab to potty weally bad."

"Okay, baby." I sped up a little since we were so close. I quickly threw the car in park and grabbed her to run into the house. “Hey, y’all..Excuse us. Running to the potty,” I yelled to my sister and Amelia as we passed them.

When we made it this little girl acted like an old woman, sighing heavily when I helped her to the toilet. “Thank you, Daddy. Ise about not made it.” I laughed. “Is Gwampa hea?”

“Yes…make sure you wash your hands.”

“Daddy…Ise not two. Ise know to wash my hands.”

“Alright, Miss Sassy……Now come on so you can meet everyone.” She dried her little hands, and then we walked back out to the living room where my sister and Amelia were sitting. “Riley, this is your Aunt Zoe. She’s my sister.”

“Hello.” Riley smiled at my sister for half a second before turning back to me. “Daddy, Ise wanna see Gwampa.”

“You will.” I can’t help but laugh. “But meet your aunt first.” She pursed her little lips before turning back to Zoe and smiling. Zoe smiled and kneeled in front of her.

“Well, hello. It’s so nice to finally meet you. I’ve heard so much about you, Riley. Can I give you a hug?” Riley looked at me and her mother before opening her arms and hugging Zoe. As soon as the hug was over, she came back to me and held onto my leg.

“Mommy, Daddy’s gonna be in twouble again.” She said to Amelia.

“Hey. I thought we were in this together.”

“Lucas, what did you do?” She tried to look mad, but the twitch in her lip gave her away.

“Build A Bear.”

“God…How much did you spend?”

“I don’t know.”

“I know…Daddy gabes the lady 5 big dollas.” Her snitching ass held up her hand like we didn’t hear her the first time.

“Lucas.” Amelia groaned.

“She said ‘pwetty pwease’, Amelia. You know I’m a sucker

for her when she says that." Before she could respond the side door opened and my parents walked in.

"Oh my word. Am I finally meeting my grandbaby?" My dad said. Riley let my leg go and went to my dad and stood in front of him. She tilted her head and looked right at him.

"Are you Gwampa?"

"I am."

"Okay. Let me see."

"Let you see what, sweetheart?" My dad asked.

"Libby at mys school say her gwampa gibs her big hugs and lollipops. Ise want some." God, she's fucking adorable. Everyone in the room awed and looked like they wanted to cry.

"Come on, sweetheart." He opened his arms. "I got you on the hug, but you're gonna have to talk to your nana about the lollipop." My dad hugged Riley tight then tickled her until she was begging him to stop. Then he whispered something into her ear. She smiled wide at whatever he said.

"What are you two whispering about?" My mother asked.

"It's a secwet, Nana. Ise can't tell ya."

"Well, don't forget about meeting your Uncle Lawson." My brother said as he came into the living room. "Hi, Riley. I'm your daddy's brother, so that makes me your Uncle Lawson."

"Umm." Riley cocked her head to the side with her finger up to her mouth like she was thinking. "Ise not like Uncle Lawsoon…Ise call you Uncle Lou Lou instead." She gasped. "Ise like it. Do you, Daddy?"

"I love it, baby." I laughed at the look on my brother's face. "Morning, Uncle Lou Lou."

I was listening to Riley talk to my dad and brother, but I was aware that my mother was talking to Zoe and Amelia. Something told me that I wouldn't like what they were talking about, but I would find out sooner or later what it was.

Ignoring whatever they were doing, I took Riley to the game room to meet my younger siblings. She was in heaven when she saw everything my mother had in there.

When I was about to head back into the living room she didn't move an inch, says, "Ise stay here, Daddy."

When I walked back out, I shrugged to everyone. "We lost her to the play room."

"Well, that's not a bad thing. She needs to be comfortable since she's staying the night without her parents." My mom said.

"What do you mean without her parents?" I asked as I looked around.

"The four of you are going to hang out tonight. Go out, have some fun, and welcome Amelia back to town properly. Don't worry. Dad and I will take good care of Riley." I hesitated for a split second too long, and my mother laid the guilt on me. "You're gonna have so much fun, Amelia. I know you haven't been out since you became a single mother and all... Enjoy yourself and take your time coming back."

I can't help but laugh, because now I know what they were over here talking about. Amelia and Zoe more than likely came up with the idea and because they knew I wouldn't agree, they brought Mom into it.

"And what's so funny?" Mom asked.

"This...this whole thing is funny but just so we're clear, now that I *actually know* about my kid, when you need to *enjoy yourself,* I will get her anytime and any day."

The smiles wiped right off their faces and not a piece of me was sorry. We're not going to brush shit under the rug and pretend like this whole thing was my fault.

Hours later we headed to a bar in the next town over that had live music and dancing. Of course, Amelia rode with me and my sister and brother rode together, as if I'm too stupid to know what my siblings were up to. Amelia was quiet on the way to the bar which was fine with me.

My brother and sister beat us to the bar since I had to make a. stop. Thankfully, they sat opposite of each other which meant Amelia and I didn't have to sit so close. I was still spiraling from last night and wanted nothing more than to have her again.

"You should ask her to dance." My brother whispered to me.

"Are you crazy? I'm not doing that."

"Why not? I don't know why you're stalling but eventually you're going to let everything go and forgive Amelia. You could never stay mad at her. You're just being stubborn. Look at her…Ask her to dance."

I turned my glass up and emptied my drink. If I dance with Amelia, I'm going to want to touch her and then that will complicate things. And I refuse to mess shit up for my daughter…but dammit if I don't want to strip that short ass dress that I'm sure she got from my sister off and fuck her senseless.

Walking away from her last night was one of the hardest things that I have ever done. I don't know if I could ever do that again. I don't know…maybe that's a good thing. My reasons for being angry at her lessen more and more every day….And how can I stay mad at her. I've never been able to because she's always owned me.

CHAPTER 15

melia

SOMETHING LAWSON WAS SAYING irritated Lucas. I watched him as he downed his drink before getting up and walking to the bar. I couldn't take my eyes off him, not even when a woman that seemed familiar to him walked up, rubbing her hands across his shoulders.

He turned around and when he saw her, his smile widened. I couldn't make out what they were saying but she was definitely flirting and as if the sight of the two of them talking didn't make my chest hurt, the tight hug he gave her did.

A hug that lasted a little long as she whispered something into his ear. Even though I had no business being jealous, I was, and it gutted me. Then, I watched as she squeezed his hand when they said goodbye. He kissed her cheek and she left.

He grabbed his drink, walked back to the table, and sat

down. He and Lawson exchanged silent words. Still, he said nothing to me or Zoe, and I knew that it was because he was irritated. It felt like we were forcing him to be around me, and I hated it. It made me want to call an Uber and leave.

"This is stupid. He won't even look at me." I whispered to Zoe. She had pulled me into her room this evening and gave me a crazy makeover. She pricked and pulled in places that had never been. She did my hair and makeup. Then, she stuffed me in this short ass dress and for what…Lucas won't even look at me.

"Girl, please. He's definitely looking. He's just trying not to. Remember what I said. Right now you're Amelia, not Riley's mother. Relax and see what happens, but no worries. I'm going to make this easier for you." She whispered before turning to Lawson. "Dance with me, big brother." She pouted at him. He quickly got up and the two of them ran off and left me and Lucas sitting at the table.

Ugh. *Be bold*, I thought to myself, and then I figured maybe I should just ask him to dance. "Lucas," I said at the same time he called my name. "Sorry. You go first."

"I…Would you like to dance?" . I nodded my head, and he reached for my hand, pulling me onto the dance floor. The song that was playing was one that I hadn't heard of before. It was neither fast nor slow. It was just right for Lucas to pull me into his arms to dance.

My body trembled from his touch, and I could barely breathe. "Relax, Amelia. It's just me." Lucas whispered. Without thinking I leaned my head in and rested on his chest. My eyes instantly closed, and I fought the urge to cry. Being in his arms felt like home to me.

We swayed back and forth for a few songs. Lucas suddenly leaned down and kissed my forehead. I lifted my head and looked up at him. He never stopped moving. I was still in his arms as he continued to sway us back and forth.

We stared into each other's eyes without saying a word. I don't know who leaned in first. All I knew was one moment we were staring at each other and the next we were kissing.

Lucas pulled away first and stared at me. He looked conflicted but then he kissed me again and again. Finally, he stopped and said, "You want to get out of here?" I nodded and that was all he needed. He pulled me all the way to his truck and helped me in.

We made it to his place in record time. At every stoplight he pulled me close to him and kissed me like he couldn't get enough.

When we made it to his house, he helped me out and we walked to the door. He paused and turned to me. "Amelia, if you walk through this door that's going to be it. I won't be able to control myself or what happens afterwards. Be very sure."

"I'm sure, Lucas. I want this." I wanted everything, is what I wanted to say but didn't. If all I can have is right now, I will take it.

He unlocked the door and then lifted me, carrying me to his room and literally tossing me on his bed. I don't know what got into me but I wanted to be seductive. I wanted to be the woman that drove him crazy.

I slowly lowered the straps on my dress while looking him in the eyes. I slid out of it, revealing my naked body underneath. Lucas groaned with lustful eyes as he continued to undress himself.

I laid back and waited, expecting him to climb in between my legs but he didn't. He parted them and brought his mouth to my clit. The first touch of his tongue almost made me come. Since I hadn't been with anyone else, this was the first time I've felt this, and it was driving me insane.

His wet tongue slid in and out of me and all around my

pussy before he went back to sucking on my clit. That was my undoing. My body trembled as I came on Lucas's tongue.

He continued to suck on my clit until my body was done shaking. Only then did he reach in his drawer for a condom and put it on. He lined himself up with my entrance and slammed into me…hard.

"Lucas." I moaned. "Oh, God." He moved in and out. This was much different from the other night. Then, he seemed to be fighting to keep control but not tonight. Tonight he's rough and untamed.

"Fuck, Amelia…Your pussy…feels…so good. Are you still flexible, baby?" Without stopping, he lifted one leg and pushed it back towards the headboard and turned his body slightly the other way.

With every thrust his body rubbed against my clit and in no time I was coming again. Only when I had come again did Lucas slow down.

He lowered my leg, brought his hands to the side of my face and kissed me passionately as he moved in and out of me. I did my best to rock with him. Our bodies moved in sync…This was different. Lucas was making love to me.

As he stared into my eyes it felt like he was baring his soul to me, and I wanted it. I wanted every piece of Lucas…mind, body, and soul…And if he allowed me to, I would give him mine. I would give him every single piece of me because nobody could ever compare to him.

We were young, and I made some stupid mistakes, but I knew it then and I know it now…I was in love with Lucas. Even when I was angry at him, I loved him. I felt it so strongly as he made love to me, saying my name over and over as I say his.

My body was climbing to the edge once again but this time when I came, he came with me. Our tongues explored each other as we moaned into each other's mouths.

When we were done, Lucas went to the bathroom to take off the condom. He came back with a towel for me. I was exhausted and as sweet as he is, he cleaned me up himself.

When he went to take the towel back I expected him to go to the living room and sleep like before. But to my surprise, he climbed into bed with me and pulled me into his arms.

He kissed my neck and squeezed me tight. “Goodnight, Amelia.”

“Goodnight, Lucas.” *I love you,* I said to myself. It was nowhere near the time for me to tell him something like that, but I will…soon.

CHAPTER 16

ucas

WAKING up with Amelia in my arms doesn't make me feel even a pinch of regret like I thought it would. It feels…right. This is how we should have always been. I've been laying here for the last hour not moving a muscle because I don't want to wake her up.

The moment that she wakes up, this little perfect bubble will pop, and I'm not sure I'm ready for it . Right now, we're just Lucas and Amelia, laying in bed after a great night hanging out with my siblings and having some good sex.

When she wakes up what will we become? Will things be awkward, or will we just ignore what's happened between us, again?

We can't. I can't keep sleeping with her knowing that feelings are involved and that everything could affect our daughter.

Holding her in my arms, I can't help but to stare down at

her beautiful face. Sometime during the night she turned toward me and wrapped her arm around me too. Looking down, I can't help but reflect over everything that's happened between us.

I've never been so angry with her in my life, but it was more so about my hurt feelings than my anger. It hurt that she would think so little of me, but in the end I understood how she could believe that she was talking to me after what she heard Bryce say.

It's not that I don't want to forgive her, but then what? What happens then? I'm not a fool. I have seen the looks she gives me when she thinks I'm not looking. The love is still there, and I definitely love her, but what if we tried to reconcile and things go wrong?

My daughter is my main priority right now, but I would be lying if I said that I didn't want this. A very big part of me wanted Amelia just as much as I had when we were younger and being a family with her and Riley would be amazing.

Amelia started to stir and stretch a bit. When she finally opened her eyes, she looked relieved before the biggest smile crossed her face. Did she think I wouldn't still be with her when she woke up? "Good morning," I said.

"Good morning." She stared at me for a moment before I couldn't help myself anymore and leaned in and kissed her. Fuck me, I couldn't help but want her. Willing myself to break the kiss, I bring my forehead to hers.

"Amelia," I whispered as I closed my eyes. I wasn't sure why I called her name. I just knew I was confused. I sighed heavily before moving to lie on my back. I could feel her eyes on me while I looked only at the ceiling.

"What's wrong, Lucas?" She asked as she sat up and the sheet slid down her body. I couldn't help the deep inhale that came from me.

"Please, pull the sheet up. I can't think with your tits out."

Because seeing them makes me want to pull them into my mouth and suck them.

"Okay, fine, but tell me what's wrong."

"I can't...I can't keep sleeping with you like you're some casual fuck I picked up at the bar. It makes me feel shitty."

"Why? And I have to say I'm going to lose it right now if you say it's because I'm Riley's mother." She said firmly.

"But you are Riley's mother, Amelia."

"Is that all you see when you look at me, Lucas? Am I only Riley's mother to you?" Her voice held a bite to it like I had done something wrong.

"I'm only trying to respect you."

"That's not what I asked you." She shook her head. "I may be Riley's mother but I'm also a woman, Lucas. I'm more than just your daughter's mother. Can't you see that?"

"I do. I do see you as more than her mother, but there's no separating who you are. If I hurt you, this woman that you're trying to be to me, will that not affect you as Riley's mother? I just got Riley in my life. I can't do anything that will fuck that up and you...You're the most important person to our daughter. I can't hurt you."

She lays back again and lets out a heavy breath before turning to me and I turn towards her. "What are we doing, Amelia?"

"I don't know. I know that I've never not wanted you, but you–" Her bottom lip trembled, and her eyes held unshed tears. "But you've gotten to a point that you hate me."

"Amelia" I reached up and wiped her tears. "I've never hated you a day in my life." If it had been anyone else I would not have cared about their tears, but Amelia wouldn't cry unless she was really hurting and upset.

"It feels that way sometimes. You're there with Riley and I'm there too but we don't talk, we don't even look at each other so yeah it feels like you hate me or at least can't stand the sight of me."

"I'm not going to lie to you, for a while it did hurt to look at you. When you left...I was fucked up for a long time. I thought...I thought maybe I had done something to you, Amelia, like maybe I forced you somehow or made you feel that you had to do something that you didn't want to. I spiraled, Amelia. I was fucked up...I was drinking and getting high, trying to do anything to shut the voice in my head telling me that I was a piece of shit and that's why you left."

"Lucas," She cried but I shook my head.

"I don't hate you, Amelia. I just had to deal with the fact that I went through so much for nothing. I got so bad that my parents had to check me into detox, Amelia, and by the time I got myself together and back on the straight and narrow, two years had passed."

"I'm sorry." She cried. "I know it's not enough, but I'm so sorry. I had no idea or I would have come back." I pulled her to me and held her while she cried. I wasn't trying to upset her or play the blame game. I just needed her to know why this was hard for me.

"What can I do?" Her voice trembled as she spoke.

"What do you mean?"

"What can I do for you to forgive me? I'm not trying to push you or rush you because I know that I was wrong and hurt you, but I don't want to let time go by when I can try to fix this. You deserved better and I failed at that. I'm sorry." The look in her eyes was so intense that I almost couldn't take it.

"I just need some time, that's all." You would have thought I said the ugliest thing to her from the way her face twisted in pain.

"I don't know if I can deal with you shutting me out. It

hurts too much, Lucas." For a moment I just stared into her eyes. I lifted my hand to wipe her tears again and she closed her eyes as more tears came.

I couldn't help myself as I kissed her eyes and then her lips. "Look at me, Amelia...You give me some time and I won't shut you out."

Amelia's POV

When I woke up and Lucas was still in bed with me, I was in heaven. I honestly thought that he would leave the bed after I fell asleep.

I was so happy that he was there until we had to talk. I completely understood where he was coming from when he said we couldn't have just casual sex. Lucas and I could never do casual sex. I know that because my heart has always been in play when it came to us.

However, I couldn't help myself but to take the little piece of him that he was offering. After our conversation today, I think I need to put the brakes on that. I've been blind to everything but my feelings and my needs. Not once did I ask him how he felt after I left and now I found out that he had been through so much.

He hasn't moved away from me yet, which is a good sign that he can at least tolerate me and my selfish idiocy. My heart screamed and ached for this beautiful man that went through so much over a complete misunderstanding.

"Amelia." Lucas's voice was soft. I looked up at him, and his thumb rubbed the tear from my eyes as he looked at me.

"I'm sorry. I just feel horrible about everything."

"I know that you feel bad but if you keep on—" His

sentence was interrupted by his phone. He reached for it and smiled when he saw who was calling. "Morning, sweet girl."

"Daddy, where are you?" Riley groaned.

"I'm at home. Where are you?"

"At Nana and Gwampa's, member? Yous left me. Yous didn't come back. Ise stayed cause Nana say yous coming back later."

"Oh...umm...I came back because Beary was home all alone. I didn't want him to be scared since you weren't going to be at home, but I will be there in a little while for breakfast." I mouthed 'liar' to him.

"Okay, Daddy. Gwampa gabes me ice cweam but him say don't tells Mommy and Nana cause Nana say Gwampa gabes me junk and he's can't do that. Gwampa say nobodys tells him what to do with him gwambaby. That's me, Daddy."

I had to cover my mouth to keep from laughing. "I know that's you. Your grandpa better not give you any sugar before breakfast."

"Byes, Daddy. Ise going back to Gwampa now." She said before ending the call.

"I do believe that she hung up on me when she realized that I wasn't on her and her grandpa's side. I'm going to get them two."

"Oh please. She's going to have you in on their mess and you know it." I laughed at him. Riley definitely has her daddy wrapped around her finger.

Lucas grunts as he stretches. "I guess we better get up. Don't want to be late for breakfast." Lucas surprised me by kissing me on the forehead and then asking me if I wanted to shower with him.

I should have said no but I couldn't. I will take any piece of Lucas that he chooses to give me right now. To my disappointment, all we did was shower. There was no shower sex or even a friendly touch. We showered, got dressed, and headed to his parent's house.

That was a week ago. It's been a week of what is supposed to be me being patient and Lucas not shutting me out. He hasn't, but it feels so forced. That's not my main problem right now though.

Yesterday my boss called me. She wanted to know when I was planning on coming back. She's been patient with me, but she needed to know if she needed to replace me.

What am I supposed to do now? I originally told her I would be back in a couple of weeks. I came to check on my mother but she's all better and back to normal. I came for my mother but stayed longer for Lucas.

He had just met his daughter and I didn't feel right about leaving so soon but now what? What am I supposed to tell him? And how will Riley take leaving her father and her many new relatives to go to a place where it's just me and her?

CHAPTER 17

ucas

My evenings have all been the same since the day I found out that Amelia and I shared a daughter. Every day, if I go to work, I fly out of the bank to go see her. I'm not naive to the fact that my days are numbered with her.

Amelia hasn't spoken much about going back to her home, but I suspect that it's been on her mind. Since we talked, things have been a little different. I promised not to shut her out and I haven't.

Every day when I spend time with Riley I have included Amelia and I can tell that she's happy about it. I would be lying if I said it didn't feel good to have some good moments with her and our daughter. It's been perfect if I'm being honest.

Today, I'm hoping to have another moment with them. The carnival is in town so I got the three of us tickets to go.

Amelia seemed surprised when I told her. She tried to hide her smile, but I could see it.

When she smiles that way, she reminds me of the old Amelia. It reminds me of how much I've always cared for her and it makes me question if I'm really willing to give that up.

I stand firm on my daughter being first in my life because I have to make up for lost time...but would it really be so bad to let things run its course and see how things end?

I will have to worry about that later because as soon as my truck hits the gravel heading to Amelia's place, Riley's bursting out the door, jumping and waving.

"Hey, Riley girl...You're excited, huh?"

"Ise so excited, Daddy," she screams, but then she starts whispering. "Mommy say her gone win me some pwizes cause yous can't do it." I swear this little girl has no loyalty. She's cool with me now but will snitch on me to her mother as soon as she gets a chance.

"Talking about me, Amelia?" I looked at her as she came out the door.

"Not really." She chuckled. "I just remember you at a carnival trying to win prizes. You have a lot of strength but no finesse."

"Hmm. My finesse is just fine and you of all people know that...very...well." I smirked at her. Her eyes widened and she nibbled her lip, looking embarrassed. "Alright, you two, let's get to the carnival."

I helped Riley get into her seat while Amelia went to her side. Once we were all in and on the way I could see how nervous she was. She was fidgeting and she only does that when something is troubling her.

Looking into the rearview mirror, I saw that Riley was occupied on her tablet. "What's wrong, Amelia?"

Her eyes snapped to mine and she stared for a moment before putting on a fake smile. "Nothing's wrong. I was just lost in my own thoughts." She was lying but I would leave her alone for now.

Riley gasped loudly from the backseat. "Daddy, Ise see it. Ise see the wides. Ise wanna go on the big one."

"Alright, but first I need to stop at some games so I can show Mommy that I can win you a prize." Amelia laughed a little.

"SERIOUSLY, Lucas. You've spent over $100 already. That's enough. Let me try." Amelia scolded me.

"Just one more time. I bet I will get it this time."

"Lucas."

"Okay…Okay. Riley, Mommy's going to win you a bear."

"Yay. Mommy's the best." She cheered. She wasn't wrong. It took Amelia one damn try and she had already won a bear for Riley.

"Oh, don't be sour, Lucas. Let's go take Riley to the big ride." Amelia smiled with pride. We walked to the ride with Riley in between us as we both held her hand.

We had to wait in line but when we finally made it inside the riding car, Riley climbed in my lap and Amelia sat to my right.

As the ride started to move I could hear Riley going on and on about everything that she could see. I could hear her, but my focus was on the beautiful, smiling woman that was beside me.

Seeing her smile at our daughter with happiness made my heart squeeze with longing. I've missed her…more than I thought I did. Without thinking, my hand moves to hold hers. She slowly looked me into my eyes for a moment without showing any emotion.

For a moment she just stared. Then, her smile returned and she squeezed my hand before turning back to Riley.

The moment was over but we stayed like that, hand in hand for the remainder of the ride. Once it was over, Riley wanted to be picked up so I carried her in one hand and grabbed Amelia's hand with the other.

For a few moments I was mentally in a good place. I didn't know if the rest of the day would be easy for us but right now it was and I was happy…until I heard a squeal of a voice.

"Oh my gosh, Lucas." Kelly, a classmate and someone I had hooked up with in the past, came walking towards us. I know Kelly and she's messy as hell. We've seen each other several times since our fling and not once has she approached me. "Goodness, is this Amelia from high school? I haven't seen you in years."

"Hi, Kelly." Amelia mumbled, the smile no longer on her face. I could see that she was now uncomfortable.

"And who is this little one?"

"Ise, Riley." And that was the end of that conversation, because I didn't want her talking to my daughter.

"Good seeing you, Kelly, but excuse me. I'm spending time with my family." I put my arm around Amelia and walked away. "Let's get some cotton candy. You want some cotton candy, Riley?"

Amelia relaxed into me as we walked and just like that she was back to normal. I won't lie and say I've been celibate while she was away, but I'll be damned if anyone will approach her or my kid.

Amelia's POV

Is it petty of me to be happy about him brushing off Kelly? Maybe but oh well. I've never liked Kelly and it's not because she had the biggest crush on Lucas. It's because she tried very hard to be the mean girl in school.

Not to me, but to others. She probably wanted to be the mean girl to me, but she was too busy trying to hop on Lucas's dick and she knew he wouldn't mess with her if she was mean to me.

As far as I know, they never hooked up in high school, but I was away for 5 years. I'm sure during that time Lucas has had his share of women. That's not my problem though and I won't make it one.

I have no right to tell him who to interact with but when he responded to her…Ahh. I fucking swooned. When he told her that he was spending time with his family, I almost jumped him right in the middle of the damn carnival.

"Why are you smiling so hard?" Lucas asked suddenly. We were currently sitting at a little table eating funnel cakes and having a drink.

"Oh nothing. I'm just enjoying myself." It wasn't a total lie. I was definitely enjoying spending time with my two favorite people.

"Mhm." Lucas hummed, knowing that I was lying. "Well, we better get going." We cleaned up our mess and headed to his truck. I walked slightly behind him so I could shamelessly ogle him while he carried our daughter.

Being out with them and enjoying our time makes me realize how stupid I was for thinking that Lucas wouldn't want his child.

Once we got to the car and Lucas buckled Riley in, we climbed into the front. For a moment, Lucas looked at me and then he looked away. Finally he spoke, "I know that Riley had fun tonight, but did you?"

"Yes. Of course. I had an amazing time. Thank you for letting me tag along." I smiled at him.

"It wasn't for you to tag along, Amelia." He reached over

and rubbed my cheek. "I wanted you there." He leaned in as he grabbed me by the neck and pulled me in close. He kissed me slowly and softly before pulling back. "Stay with me tonight...you and Riley. Stay at my place."

"Okay." I mumbled. "And maybe we can talk later. I have something I need to discuss with you." I said nervously. I was unsure of how Lucas would react to the conversation about us going home but I was sure it wouldn't be good.

"I know we need to talk. I can tell that you have something on your mind but for now, let's get our little sleeping baby girl home." *Home*. Oh how I wish that this was a perfect world with Lucas as my husband and us sharing a home.

I must have fallen asleep during the quick ride back to his place because I didn't even realize that we had arrived. When I woke up, Lucas was lifting me from the truck and carrying me through his house.

"Sorry. I can walk." I said as my eyes fluttered open.

"It's fine. We're almost there."

"Where's Riley?"

"I put her to bed already. She's tired so I washed her face and feet. She can bathe in the morning."

"You're such a good dad, Lucas." I meant it. He attends to Riley's needs like he's been doing it since day one.

When we made it to Lucas's room, he laid me on the bed. Then he took off my clothes and shoes and pulled the cover up over me.

He rubbed my hair and then kissed my forehead. "Goodnight." He moved to walk away but I grabbed his hand.

"Where are you going? Stay with me, please."

CHAPTER 18

ucas

Do I still have a hard time when it comes to my feelings on missing my daughter's first years? Yes, but I know without a doubt that I want Riley in my life as well as Amelia. I won't fight it anymore, but I also won't set myself up for more heartache.

"Amelia, if I stay with you I'm not going to hold back. You said we needed to talk and I'm assuming this is about you leaving. I can't go all in if I'm here and you're there. I'm going to always do my best for Riley, but if you want things to go further with us, you need to be sure about it. Think long and hard about how you want to handle things going forward. Until then, I'm going to shower."

I wasn't in the shower for 5 minutes when my shower door opened and Amelia stepped in, naked and beautiful. "Amelia." I groaned.

"I don't know what will happen after this. We will have to

make plans for that, but I know one thing, Lucas MacArthur…If you're willing to open your heart for me, I'm going all in with you." She said before wrapping her arms around my neck and kissing me roughly.

"Mmm…Are you sure? I want you to be sure."

"I'm sure." I lifted her in my arms. As she wrapped her legs around my body I entered her fast and hard. "Oh, Lucas." She moaned.

"Mmm." I moved her back to the wall and slammed into her over and over. "You're mine, Amelia…Never leave me again." I moaned before kissing her again.

I slowed my pace but just a little. I wanted to feel all of her as she felt every inch of me. We didn't have everything figured out or even a little bit figured out but from this moment forward, this woman was mine.

I was done waiting and done dealing with the what ifs. What I wanted more than anything was for Amelia to finally be mine…forever and I wanted to make her feel what I felt.

I went from fucking her hard to making love to her slowly and just as she came, she moaned, "I'm never leaving you again, Lucas. I love you." I came right after her with her name on my lips.

I kissed her lips before pulling back and looking into her eyes. "I love you too, Amelia." I whispered. "I love you."

After catching our breath, we released each other and then actually showered. We washed each other's bodies, stealing kisses and sweet moments staring into each other's eyes.

When we were finally done and dried off, we walked to my bed hand in hand. I pulled her into my arms intending on going to sleep, but Amelia had other plans.

She climbed on top of me and lowered herself onto my dick. It felt too good, too raw, and too real.

It wasn't until both of us came and Amelia collapsed into

my arms that I realized it felt different because we hadn't used protection nor did we use any in the shower. "Amelia, we didn't use–"

"I know. I didn't think about it until I was almost there and I couldn't stop. We should be fine. It was only twice. I don't know how you feel, but I'm definitely not ready for another baby."

"I mean, I wouldn't be mad if you ended up pregnant, but I would definitely prefer to wait so I will make sure to be more careful. I just feel like I owe it to Riley to spend some time with her before thinking about having another kid. I want to give her my all…and you. I want to give you my all too." I admitted.

"Me too, Lucas. Me too."

Amelia's POV

This morning I should be feeling extremely happy after what Lucas and I said to each other last night. Unfortunately, morning is here and reality has set in and I pretty much promised him we would work things out.

It was impulsive and while I want nothing more than for everything to work out, what happens now.

I feel Lucas starting to stir behind me so I turn over to face him. His eyes are still closed but he moves his lips to kiss my head. "Good morning." His voice was raspy and so fucking sexy.

"Morning."

"How long have you been awake?"

"Not long."

"Mhm. Let me guess, you're regretting last night." He slowly opened his eyes when I hesitated.

"I'm not regretting it. I'm just trying to figure some things out. We still need to talk as well."

"Well, I'm here now. Talk." He says as his arms loosen on me and he sits up and faces me.

"My boss contacted me the other day. She said she needed a date for my return. With me missing so many days, they've been short handed."

"And what did you tell her?"

"Nothing yet. I wasn't sure what to tell her. I didn't want to take Riley away from you, but I can't keep my job waiting."

"Last night when I told you that I couldn't go all in with you unless you were sure, I meant that. I know it's not fair to ask you to move back home but–" He shrugs.

If I'm being honest, it makes more sense for me to move home than for us to do long distance or for him to move with me. Lucas helps to run his family bank, they have several family businesses here, and he has purchased a townhome. I would have help here with his big family and my mother. Things would ultimately be easier for me.

Back home, it's just me and we live in a small two bedroom apartment. Don't get me wrong, I love my place that I managed to make it a home for the two of us, but it does get hard and lonely sometimes.

I work hard at a local daycare, which I love doing, but I only started working there because I could take Riley. With help I could maybe change jobs and do something that I really love, but— "What if we do this and it doesn't work out? Then what, because uprooting my life for nothing would be horrible."

"Amelia." He groaned with his face scrunched up like he wanted to go off on me. "What the h—"

"Daddy." Riley squealed as she came into the room. Thankfully while we were talking I slipped on his shirt and he slipped on some shorts. Otherwise Riley would be getting an eye full.

"Morning, sweet girl. You're up early."

"I wanna talk to Uncle Lou Lou." She pouted.

"It's kind of early, Riley. You can call your Uncle Lou Lou in a little while. How about some breakfast until then? Wanna help me make Mommy some pancakes?"

"Yes and Ise wants some eggs and bacon too."

"Okay. You go wash your hands and I will be right behind you." He said to Riley. As she ran off he looked back at me. "We will finish this conversation later."

That was all he said before turning and walking away. Somehow I feel like I've made things worse. I made promises that I should have thought through first and now he thinks I was just bullshitting him.

Of course he does. He told me that if last night happened he was going all in. He gave me a choice and I made my bed. Now I either have to lie in it or knock it down all together. Jesus Christ, Amelia. Get it together.

Lucas

Amelia confuses the fuck out of me. She's been wanting me to forgive her and give her a chance but now that I am, she's shifty as fuck.

I can't go there with her until she's sure of what she wants. I told her this and she agreed. I don't know, maybe it was the heat of the moment for her but fuck that. It's not fair to me.

So, I'm gonna have to step back. I will not start things back up with her when she can so easily hang her love over my head just to snatch it back when she gets ready to.

"Daddy. The pancakes."

"Shit. Sorry, Riley. I will make more." I was so busy thinking about Amelia that I burned the batch of pancakes. "Just give me a second and I will have another batch ready."

I finished with breakfast and we ate in silence other than Riley talking about calling her Uncle Lou Lou.

"Alright, Riley. You go and talk to your Uncle Lou Lou. I'm going to get ready so I can take you and your mother home." I dialed my brother's number and gave Riley the phone.

Thirty minutes later I'm done and walking out my bedroom. Amelia and Riley were both dressed. "Ready to go?" I asked them. Amelia nodded her head slowly. I didn't know what the look on her face meant and honestly, I didn't care at the moment.

"Ise don't wanna leabe, Daddy. Why can't me and Mommy stay with you?"

"You can come back anytime you want, but Mommy and I will have to talk about that later." Her little face fell. Then she hopped down off the couch, grabbed her little bag, and walked to the door.

I don't want them to leave and I hate that I'm disappointing my daughter but I can't deal with Amelia right now. I'm sure she would love to stay here but then what? She wakes up the next morning and regrets it again.

The car has never been so quiet as we rode back to her place. We didn't say a word, not even Riley. I looked in the rearview mirror and saw Riley looking out the window with her lip poked out and her eyes glossy with tears.

Fuck. What am I going to do if Amelia decides to leave? I can't be away from my little girl.

The short ride felt long as fuck. When we finally pulled into the driveway, Riley started to cry so loud and hard that you would think someone had hurt her.

"Riley, what's wrong?" Amelia asked as we parked and started to get out.

"Ise not wanna leabe my daddy." She wrapped her arms around my neck so tight when she was unbuckled.

"You've left me before, Riley, but you've never been so upset. Is something wrong?"

"Mommy say we's habe to go. Ise heard her on the phone. I don't wanna leabe." Amelia gasped and looked at me and Riley wide eyed.

"Lucas, that's not what I meant. I was on the phone with my boss and I guess she overheard something and got confused."

"Mmm…Riley, don't cry, okay. I will always see you. I don't care how far I have to come, okay." I rubbed her back and held her until she finally calmed down. "Now run in and clean your face. Call me later."

After I was sure Riley couldn't hear me, I turned to Amelia. "Judging by the look on your face, you were not going to tell me about you talking to your boss. That's fine. Do what you want but I will see my daughter. Do me a favor and at least have the decency to let me know when you leave this time because if I have to hunt you down to see my child, you won't like me anymore…that's something that I can guarantee you."

CHAPTER 19

melia

THINGS WERE NOT the same between me and Lucas, and I have no one to blame but myself. He finally opened his heart up to me and in true Amelia fashion, I fucked it up. I mean it was less than a damn day.

He was right, I was never going to tell him about that conversation, but it wasn't because I was trying to take Riley from him. It was just because I wasn't sure how to handle things but the more I thought about it, the more I realized that I didn't want to leave or to take Riley away from Lucas.

The problem was now he isn't giving me the time or space to speak with him about it. When he comes over and sees Riley, he barely says a word to me and he is sure to leave before Riley is in bed.

There's a knock and the door. I rushed to the door to keep whoever it was from waking up Riley. She's been really moody since she overheard my conversation that day. When I opened the door, Mrs. MacArthur was standing there.

"Hey, Mrs. MacArthur."

"Hello, sweetheart. How are you feeling?"

"I'm doing okay. My mother's out if you all were supposed to get together."

"Oh, I know. I actually came over to speak with you if you have a moment."

"Sure. We can speak in the living room." I take a seat and she sits right next to me and turns to look me square in the eyes.

"Now, how are you really doing? How are things going with you, Riley, and Lucas?"

"Lucas and Riley are amazing. He's a wonderful father." She smiled with pride.

"He is, but I meant everyone. You all were spending some family time together, but I haven't been seeing that and I just wanted to make sure that things were okay." I decided to go with the truth.

"I've messed up with him again. He told me up front that he couldn't go there with me unless I was sure about us. I agreed and he opened his heart back to me. I do want that but I told him that I may have to go back because what if things don't work out and then things could get bad with us co-parenting."

"So, he's pulled away?"

"He has. I don't even get the time to talk to him. He's all about Riley now."

"Do you love him? And I don't mean the boy him or the father of your child. Do you love my son and want to spend your life with him?"

"Yes, I do. Seeing how torn up he and Riley have been has taken my doubt away. I know that we would do whatever it takes to work things out because he can't be away from Riley and I can't be away from him."

"Then do whatever it takes to fix it."

"I don't know how to fix it."

"Think about it. Despite the time apart, you know Lucas better than anyone else. What could you do to make him understand that you want him? Think about it and make it happen."

We talked for a long time but my thoughts were too cloudy to be engaged in the conversation. What she said made sense. I did need to make things right with Lucas. He may not want to talk to me or be around me but somehow I had to make him see that I meant it...that he can trust my word about loving him.

I thought about what she said all afternoon. I didn't have a clue what I could do and then suddenly it hit me. I knew what would make him know that I not only wanted him now but I've wanted him the whole time...even when I was pregnant with Riley.

Lucas's POV

"Lucas...You're not even listening to me." My brother's annoying ass sighed heavily, breaking me out of my never-ending thoughts of Amelia and Riley. It's been a long fucking two days for me and my baby girl.

Every day my routine has been the same since I found out she was mine. I would leave and go hang out with Riley, but I've been busy with work. So, it's been a lot of phone calls and promises of what we will do this weekend when she comes over because by the time I am off, she's asleep.

Amelia and I haven't talked much but not for lack of

trying on her part. I'm not interested in hearing any excuses from her, nor am I interested in letting her play with my feelings while she figures out hers.

So, right now and until I decide that I can deal with her shit...I'm focusing on my daughter. I'm not trying to be an asshole, but it is what it is.

I'm brought out of my thoughts once again when my brother clears his throat. "My bad, go on." He looks at me like I had lost my mind before continuing.

"I was saying, asshole, that it's going to take a lot of work to get Taylor's building the way it needs to be done. I agree with her that it's a perfect spot for a bakery, but the renovations are going to take me longer than the 3 weeks that we were shooting for. Then once that's done, we have to do the actual designs and get everything set up the way she wants it."

"I thought you said it was a simple job which is why you said it would take about 3 weeks."

"I thought so too, but then she came up with some crazy but good ideas and I think she should do them. So, it's probably going to take an extra month."

"Shit.

"I know, but keep in mind that I'm working with just a few of the guys because of the different projects going on right now."

"Gotcha. Well, that may not be so bad since it will be going into the holiday season. That may be a good start for her when she's able to open. Let me know if she needs anything because she won't. She didn't even want to take the check."

"I know. She told me about it and also gave me shit about the cheap rate that we're charging her for repairs. It took some convincing for sure."

"And how did you manage to convince her, Uncle Lou Lou?" I smirk.

"Asshole." He grunts. When Riley called him the other day she said her 'Uncle Lou Lou was with a girl.' After describing the woman and her uncle's house, I knew exactly who she was referring to. "It's nothing like that. She's Trinity's little sister."

"She's a grown woman too."

"I'm not having this conversation with you." He started to get up and grabbed his things to leave.

"That's fine. You are my last meeting anyway. I'm headed out to finally see Riley after the last two days of missing her."

"Alright. Tell her that her Uncle Lou Lou says not to forget our hang out day."

"Will do." I headed out to the car, shooting Amelia a text to let her know that I was off early and was on the way.

Amelia never responded to my message and as I pulled into the long driveway I could see that her car wasn't there. Figuring she may have left to run an errand, I got out hoping that Riley was still there.

I knocked a few times and just when I was about to turn around and walk away, Amelia's mother answered the door. "Hey. How's your day been?" I said as I stepped inside.

"It's been well, although it's a little quiet around here."

"Quiet? Riley took it easy on y'all today, huh?"

"Oh, no. She isn't here."

"Oh. I was hoping she was here. Did Amelia have an errand to run?" She looked at me confusingly before sitting down in her chair.

"Lucas, Amelia and Riley are gone home."

"Gone home as in—"

"Home. They left this morning."

CHAPTER 20

melia

For days I pondered over how to make things right between Lucas and I and also with my job and everything back home.

For the last five years my life has been away from Forest View. It may not have been extravagant, but I created a safe environment for Riley and me. We had lots of love there, but now things are different.

Lucas was in her life, and although I don't deserve it, I wanted him in mine too. Lucas was an amazing father to Riley. Thinking back to the first day that I got here, I was so afraid.

I knew that it was a possibility that I would run into Lucas when I came back. I imagined a lot of things happening, but never did I imagine that what I thought was the truth was a lie.

I would have never guessed that Lucas would meet his daughter on his own and actually want her. I would have never guessed how he went from a single bachelor to being everything that his daughter could possibly need.

Riley deserves that. She deserves to have her father around and all of her family. As scary as it is I know that tearing them apart is the last thing I want to do, but now what?

Yesterday, my mother and I sat down and had a long talk. I know that I needed to right all of my wrongs and that started with her. I had a wonderful mother during my entire life and because of a mistaken issue, I abandoned her.

I spoke to her a lot and I sent her pictures but for years my mother didn't see me, and she didn't deserve that. If I'm being completely honest, if it wasn't for Mrs. MacArthur, I have no idea how long I would have stayed away.

So, I wanted to apologize to her first. Riley had settled down for her nap, so I took that opportunity to invite my mother to sit with me. "How are you, Ma?" As she took her seat at the table, I busied myself with fixing us some tea and some blueberry scones that I had made that morning.

"I'm doing so much better. Doctor says I'm in good shape. Maybe I just needed to see my girl." She smiled softly and patted my hand.

"Yeah, maybe so. I'm so sorry, Ma, that it took me so long to come back home. You have always been so amazing to me and I'm really sorry that I didn't handle things better."

"Well, sweetheart, the pain of a broken heart can cloud your judgment. Trust me, I know." The sadness in my mother's eyes hurts my heart. It's been so many years and yet somehow she never got over my father.

"It did, but I'm still sorry. You're my rock, Ma. I wish I could get back that with you and experience it all with you. I was just so afraid that you would tell the MacArthurs and I didn't want them to make Lucas do anything. Now I wish I would have come clean."

"Speaking of Lucas...are you still sticking with the decision that you made the other day?"

"Yes, I think I am."

"And you're sure that's what you want?"

"It's a lot to deal with, but yes. I've never been more sure in my life."

"Then stand firm on your decision and do what you have to do." That was the last thing my mother said before standing and hugging me tight.

Her vote of confidence was all I needed to do what I had to. That's how I ended up where I am now, on the road with Riley in tow. Hopefully by the end of the day, things will be just as they should be.

Lucas's POV

Fucking Amelia. I'm about to lose my fucking mind right now. I warned Amelia not to run off without me knowing. She could have said anything. "Hey, asshole. I'm leaving and taking your kid." Fucking something.

As I climbed back into the car, my first thought was to hit the road and go straight to her place. Call it whatever you want, but when she showed up without any details on where she had been all this time with my baby, I had someone look into it.

I didn't trust her and it's a good fucking thing I didn't or I would have no idea where to look. I at least know where to go and then we can hash this shit out, but first, I needed to stop and let my mother know that I won't be around this weekend.

This was supposed to be a good weekend for my family. My mother had planned on having a gathering with some relatives and close friends to introduce Riley to the rest of her family. Now that won't be happening.

I pulled up to my parents' house and tried to calm myself before going in. I don't know why I even tried because when it comes to her children, Marie doesn't miss a beat.

"Lucas, what's wrong?" She asked as I walked through the door.

"I'm going to possibly miss the weekend events. I have to head out of town. I'm about to leave now." I said with as much control as possible.

"Oh. What's out of town?"

"Riley."

"What?"

"Riley. Amelia left, Ma. She didn't even tell me."

"That can't be right."

"It is. I just left her house. Her mother said she was heading home."

"But when I spoke to her she seemed sure that she wanted you all to be together. I believed her."

"You can do that, but I warned Amelia that if she took Riley without speaking to me that it would be a problem. I meant that." I squeezed my eyes and touched my temple with my index finger.

"Goodness. Are you having migraines again?...Evan." She called for my dad.

"Mom, I'm fine. Seriously." I wasn't fine, but there was no need for her to call my dad. Although I'm grown she still freaks out when I get a migraine. Sure, they could be bad as shit, but right now I knew a pain that's worse.

"Yes, Love. What's wrong?" My dad asked as he came into the kitchen in a panic at the sound of my dramatic ass mother.

"He's upset and he's having a migraine. It's been a while since he had one."

"Lucas?" He looked at me with questioning eyes. I knew what he was asking without him saying it. He wanted to know if I was back heavily drinking because that was when the migraines started. After everything that I put them through I can't even be mad at the implication.

"No, Dad. I will be okay. I will call you both in the morning."

"But the weather is supposed to get bad in a little while. I don't want you on the road while it's raining."

"I will be fine, Mom. Nothing you can say will change my mind." I said more firmly than I intended to, but right now her mama bear mode wasn't helping me.

"Well, at least let me fix you a plate and give you some medicine. Please, son." I really needed to leave, but if it would ease the worried look from my mom's eyes I would agree.

"Fine, mom, but I'm leaving in 20 minutes." If I didn't put her on a time schedule she would keep me here all night.

She walked over to my dad and whispered something to him. His eyebrows furrowed as he stepped back and looked at her. "Woman, are you crazy?"

"Yes. Yes, I am and if you don't do what I asked you to, you're going to find out how crazy I am."

"Marie." He warned in a tone that I don't hear from him often. Mom has always been feisty, but Dad wasn't for the bullshit.

"Please, Evan." She said in a softer tone. He stared at her for a second before kissing her on the forehead and walking away.

"Mom, are you coming or not?"

"Yeah. Coming." She busied herself while I sat down at the table, taking out my phone to try and call Amelia. Of course I didn't get an answer and I honestly didn't expect to. It didn't matter though because within the next 3 and a half hours I will be there and she will have no choice but to speak to me.

"Here you go. Eat up." My dad came back in as I was eating and brought my mother's bag. She handed me a pill. "It's just something for your migraine."

"Thanks, Ma." I ate in silence after that. The thoughts and worry that ran through me was enough without trying to have a conversation.

Half way through my plate I started to feel really tired. Tired or not, I was determined to make my way to Riley. It was only a 3 hour drive so I wasn't worried, but then my eyes started to close.

As I struggled to keep my eyes open, I could hear my mother talking to my dad clearly. "Evan, help him to his bedroom. He will be out for the night."

Something for the migraine, my ass, was the last thing I remember thinking.

CHAPTER 21

melia

My trip home was a fucking disaster. I left my mother's house on a mission. I had things that I needed to take care of, and I had planned to get back the same day, but things didn't work out as planned.

For starters, Riley whined and cried the whole way which was the cause of me pulling over a few times, not including the two bathroom breaks that she needed.

I couldn't be upset with her though. She wanted her dad and in the beginning she thought she wouldn't see him anymore. After I explained to her that she would, she did good riding the rest of the way.

It took me a few hours to do what I needed to do and to grab some things that I needed. All of that went fine, but the ride back...Ugh. It was worse than the ride home.

Half way through the ride, just smack dab in the middle of nowhere, I got a flat tire. Of course, I didn't have a fucking signal to call anyone and to make matters worse it was pouring down raining.

I had crept my way to where I was, but it would have been dangerous for me to try to change my tire in the pouring rain so I waited it out.

It took almost two hours for it to slow enough for me to see. I wasn't near anything, but I could see up ahead that there was a gas station. If I didn't have Riley I would have walked, but she had fallen asleep.

Finally a truck stopped. An older man got out and helped me. He changed my tire and because it was getting late, he directed me to a motel that was safe.

My phone service was still shitty so I tried calling Lucas from the hotel phone, but he didn't answer. It was late and I was exhausted so I said fuck it, called it a day, and got some sleep.

At the first sign of daylight, I was pulling out and finishing my drive which was only an hour now. As I pulled in the driveway, I could see my mother's front door opening. She looked surprised to see me, which was weird.

"Morning, Ma."

"Amelia." She gaped at me. "I thought you were going home."

"I did, but I said I would be back." I said as I walked past her to go and lay Riley down. When I came back out, I could see that she was troubled about something. "What's wrong, Mama?"

"I…I didn't know you were coming back. When you said you had to go back to take care of business, I thought you would be awhile. Lucas…he came by yesterday. I told him you were gone."

"Oh, God. He must think I left. I will be back." It was early as shit, but I had to talk to him. I hope he's okay.

I jogged over to his parents' house and as I made it to the

top of the steps I could see his mother walk to the door. The big door was already open. She opened the screen and stepped into the doorway. "Amelia."

"Good morning, Mrs. MacArthur. I really need to talk to Lucas."

"Here's the thing, Amelia. When you left here the first time, I didn't step in. I try to let my children work out their own battles, but it was the worst decision that I've made as a parent. Lucas spiraled out of control. Mentally he wasn't okay." She took a deep breath before continuing while I tried to keep my shit together.

"He drank a lot, he got into fights, got pulled over several times, and even totaled a car after a night of partying. I thought I would lose my son as he spent night after night drinking and drowning out his pain of losing you. It's how he lost his chance to play ball in college." It was painful to hear it, but I deserved it.

"Finally, after I begged and pleaded with him, he allowed us to help him. He got himself together and is the man you see today. Now, Amelia, I love you. I always have and I always will, but you need to think long and hard before you walk over this threshold to my son again, because this time I will not take things lightly."

With that she closed the door and turned to leave, leaving me there in my thoughts. The thing is, I didn't need to think. I knew that I wanted Lucas. I didn't leave this time to hurt him or to stay away. I left to make things right.

I couldn't fault her for how she felt. I couldn't imagine watching Riley go through something like that and not being able to fix it.

I walked back to my mother's place with my heart heavy and mind cloudy. I walked to the back room and watched Riley sleep for a moment before lifting her in my arms and carrying her.

"Come on, Riley. Let's go take care of your daddy."

Lucas's POV

Everything fucking hurts as I start to wake up. I'm still sort of tired though which is why I don't immediately open my eyes.

At first I think I'm hearing shit because I could hear my tv playing a kid's show and I wouldn't put it past me since all night my dreams were filled with my daughter.

I was awake but still tired, so I laid there for a minute with my eyes still closed, stretching. Suddenly someone literally opened my eyes with their fingers. As my eyes started to adjust all I could see was a big smile and chubby cheeks.

"Daddy! Yous wake." Riley yelled, waking me up instantly. I pulled her to me and hugged her tight.

"Hey, baby girl. Where have you been, huh?" I started tickling her.

"Stop, Daddy. Ise came back." She said in between giggles. I continued tickling her until I heard a noise at the door. I looked up to see Amelia standing there with a smile on her face.

Instantly, my mood went from amazing to shit. She may have brought my little girl back, but her lack of communication still makes me want to show my ass, I just wouldn't do it in front of Riley.

The door widened to reveal my mother standing there. "How are you feeling, Lucas?"

"How do you think I feel, Ma? What was that you gave me because it sure wasn't something for a headache?"

"I just needed you to rest." She said unapologetically

before turning to Riley. "Riley Girl, come with Nana so your mommy and daddy can talk."

"But, Nana, Ise wanna stay with mys daddy." I wasn't too happy about being away from her right now either, but I did need to speak with Amelia.

"Daddy's really hungry, Riley, and I don't smell any food. Maybe you can help Nana make some muffins."

"Okay, Daddy. Tells yous tummy to hab patient cause Ise neber made muffins before." She sassed as she walked out of the door with my mother, leaving me and Amelia alone.

For a minute or so I stayed silent. I knew that if I talked first I was going to say some shit that I no doubt would regret. Just when I was about to speak, Amelia finally spoke first.

"Lucas, I am so sorry about everything. I never meant for it to seem like I was leaving with Riley, that wasn't what I was doing. I thought I was doing the right thing."

"By taking my child away when I asked you to communicate." I groaned.

"No. I had planned to be back before you got off."

"It still doesn't make sense, Amelia. Why didn't you just pick up the phone and call me or text and let me know that you were leaving."

"I don't know. I'm not trying to make excuses, but I'm not good at this, making good choices and having my shit together. I never was good at it. I was good at one thing, fucking shit up. It was you who always cleaned up my messes behind me, but now the mess I've made is with you and I'm trying to figure it out on my own."

"Not to be an asshole, but you're doing a poor ass job of it." It was an asshole thing to say, but I meant it and wouldn't be taking it back.

Amelia is a grown fucking woman. Surely she knows it is

a bad idea to leave without so much as a text or message through the family gossip train.

"I know that, Lucas." She said as her chin started to wobble from her holding in her tears. "I thought the best thing to do would be to head home and make things right so when I came to you I could let you know that Riley and I are moving back for good."

"What? You're staying?"

"We are." She nodded her head. "After some deep thought, I realized that I never wanted to leave you again. I couldn't imagine taking Riley away from you. I don't want to be away from you either. I know that I have a lot to work on, but I want to try, Lucas. I'm so sorry for my stupidity, but I truly went back to take care of things so that chapter was closed on my life."

I should be happy, but honestly, I'm not. The main reason is because I don't trust a word that she's saying. I don't know if and when I can completely forgive her.

I can admit that I was about ready to do that before all of this, but I was sick of Amelia's lack of consideration for me as Riley's father. I needed more than her word on this. I needed to know that this, a family with me and Riley, was what she truly wanted.

I don't want some half assed scary love or hesitant love. If she was jumping in with me, it was all or nothing. Until I can get that, I will take nothing.

CHAPTER 22

melia

LUCAS WASN'T GOING to give me a chance, I could see that. I could also see that it wasn't because he didn't want to. He just didn't trust me not to hurt him again. I can't be mad at that because Lord knows my actions have hurt him more than once, but I hope that I can prove to him that I wanted this.

"I...I have something for you if that's okay." He didn't respond to let me know whether it was okay or not, so I just got up and grabbed the box that I had sitting in the corner.

Nervously, I sat the box down on the bed next to him and opened it. His eyes followed my every movement until they landed on the box and saw the small bags with labels on them.

He looked through them with his eyebrows furrowed, no doubt trying to understand what he was looking at. I reached in and found the bag labeled number one. "Here. Open it." He opened the bag and pulled out a little onesie, a hospital bracelet, and a note.

He lifted the onesie to his face and sniffed the scent. His eyes instantly filled with tears. "It still smells like a baby."

I passed him bag after bag, giving him the chance to see how his little girl grew over the first year of her life.

The first note that I wrote was a hard one for me. I was so heartbroken but hopeful that Lucas would come around to being there. Of course I didn't know what I know now. I remember every piece of that letter.

Lucas,

Hi. I don't know if you will ever get a chance to read this, but I hope you do. I've just had our little girl. She's so beautiful, but it hurts to see how much she looks like you knowing that she may never know you. My pregnancy with her was rough. I didn't have any health issues, but it was rough because I wanted you there so bad. If you ever do get to read this or any of the others that I plan to write, I hope you can tell how much you're missed. When it was time to deliver her, I hoped for a miracle that you would somehow change your mind, but you didn't. So as best as I could, alone, I came in and had her. She made things easy for me. Just a few pushes and she was here. I hope it's okay, but I named her Riley Marie. I wanted her to have a piece of your family even if she doesn't know you. I'm hoping in some way this is the only letter that I have to write, but if not, I will talk to you again in a month.

Love always, Amelia.

It was not the only letter that I had to write. In the beginning, I wrote to him every month with updates about her milestones. After her first birthday where the two of us spent it at home over her little round birthday cake, I changed my updates to once a year.

So every year after celebrating her birthday, I would spend my night writing to him with updates about her.

"What's this Amelia? You wrote these to me?"

"Yes. I wrote them because I had always hoped that you would be there. I wanted you to see and feel everything that you missed. I have always wanted you, Lucas, especially after I found out the truth. I was just afraid of the possibility of us failing, because I can't lose you twice."

His face looked tortured as he looked at me like he wasn't sure whether I was being truthful or not. "This was my main reason for leaving, Lucas. I wanted to get this book and all of the things that I saved for you so you would know how I have always wanted you with me. I figured while I was there, I may as well talk to my boss to let her know that I wouldn't be returning and I also set up a moving company to pack my things. On the way back I got a flat in the middle of nowhere and I didn't have a signal so we stayed the night. I know that it was stupid of me not to tell you up front. I'm sorry."

I didn't know what else I could say to convince him that I wasn't trying to hurt him. I'm not surprised that it would be hard for him to believe though. My actions and uncertainty have done a number on his trust in me. No matter what though, I wouldn't give up. He deserves so much better, but I hope that he gives me a chance anyway.

Lucas's POV

Being able to see, feel, and smell Riley's baby clothes was overwhelming. It doesn't compare to actually being able to be there, but fuck if it didn't feel good to be able to smell my baby and imagine how things would have been as I read Amelia's letters.

I'm torn. My heart has always wanted Amelia even when I fought to keep my feelings at bay. I've never not wanted her, but I can't allow myself to do the back and forth shit. She promised me before that she was all in just to change her mind. I don't know if I'm ready yet.

"What's in the book, Amelia?" Her face was full of pain, but I could tell that it wasn't about her. She was genuinely concerned for me and honestly, it did my heart some good. It wasn't about seeing her hurting, it was the fact that it hurt her to know how much she hurt me and that showed how much she cared.

She pulled the book out of the box and placed it in my lap as she scooted in closer. She opened it to the first page and it was filled with pictures of her stomach as it grew each month.

As I flipped through the pages and pages of Riley I could barely contain myself. Amelia had someone take pictures of Riley's birth. There were pictures of all her firsts…first bath, first taste of food, first tooth, the first time she crawled, the first time she walked, and more. It was all there.

"I've always wanted it to be us as a family, Lucas. Everything in that box I saved to show you one day. I can be an idiot sometimes, and I don't always make the best choices, but if you give me just one more chance, I can prove to you that I will never give you a reason to doubt me again."

"And what if I say no?" Her eyes widened, and her lip started to tremble.

"I will respect your choice, but I won't stop showing you that I meant what I said. Riley and I would get a place and settle in. You and I will co-parent. Whatever you choose, I will respect it even if it's not what I want." She shrugged.

Of course I wanted to be with Amelia and my daughter,

but I was curious about her answer. Amelia is so used to me just giving in to her and her needs. I wanted to know how she would take it if I told her that I didn't want this.

I expected her to try and guilt trip me and do that pouting shit that she does. Knowing Amelia, she probably doesn't even realize that she does it, but she definitely knows how to play me. That pout and laying her forehead on my chest gets me every time.

Call me a foolish idiot because I should be telling Amelia no, but I can't. I've loved her forever and can't give up on the opportunity to have her and my daughter together. I didn't want one without the other.

"Alright, Amelia." Her eyebrows furrowed.

"Alright? What does that mean?"

"It means that I want you too." She flew into my arms so hard that she knocked me over. I wrapped my arms around her as I fell back and held her close, hoping that this is the last time that we have to go through anything like this.

She cried in my arms for a moment. When she calmed down, she slowly raised her head to look at me. I leaned down and kissed her soft lips. Fuck, I missed these lips.

The past week or so, I stopped being so affectionate with her because I didn't know where this would go. So, not only do I miss kissing her lips, I miss burying my dick deep inside of her.

It showed too. I kissed her over and over until those soft kisses became passionate, sloppy ones. I was well aware that we weren't home, but at the moment I didn't give a shit.

I trailed my hand down her body. Just as I was about to climb on top of her, my door burst open. I completely forgot the fucking door wasn't locked.

A loud gasp came from Riley. "Daddy, yous kissing Mommy."

"I am kissing Mommy." Now that we will be together as one family, I didn't want to hide anything from her.

"Oh yes, yes, yes. Come on, Daddy, yous can eat yous bweakfast. Ise gotta go tell mys Uncle Lou Lou that Ise habing a baby bwother."

What the fuck?

Amelia's POV

"What the hell is she talking about?" I looked at Lucas as Riley skipped out of the room. That little girl says whatever comes to her mind.

"I have no idea, but let's go eat. We have a lot to do today."

"Oh. What do you mean?"

"Well, we have to move you and Riley's stuff in my place, well, our place now."

"You want me to move in with you?" I was genuinely surprised. I thought he would want to date a while and see how things went before we took another step. I figured he wouldn't trust me enough to move forward yet.

"I do. We're going to be together, Amelia. There is no backing out now. Once I have you and Riley in my hold, there's no letting you go. Everything else we will figure out later." He leaned down and kissed me. "Including Riley and her baby brother."

He walked away, leaving no room for me to respond and leaving me stunned in the process. I awkwardly walked out to the kitchen where everyone else was already fixing their plates.

I'm usually so comfortable with the MacArthurs, but after the morning I've had with Mrs. MacArthur, I'm not sure how everyone else is going to feel. Not that I blame any of them. but I just don't want to intrude on their family time.

"Amelia, what are you doing? Come on before the food gets cold." Lucas said.

"Umm...maybe I should go home and come back later."

"Why?"

"I don't want to upset anybody. Your mother was pretty upset earlier. I can just come back later."

"No."

"What?"

"I said no. I have no idea what conversation you and my mother had, but my family loves you. They wouldn't hold a grudge against you for anything. You say you want to be with me, then prove it. You can't just love me when everything is convenient and calm for you. Love me when it's hard too. So, no. You don't get to walk out that door because you may or may not feel awkward for a few minutes."

He's right of course. I have a bad habit of not facing my shit. You would think that I would have learned from when I ran from him before. I reached for his hand and nodded my head. I couldn't speak. The lump in my throat wouldn't allow me to.

We settled down and ate breakfast with the rest of his family. There was some tension in the room, but it wasn't because of me. Zoe had brought Bryce with her and of course Lucas was still fuming from that whole thing.

After we were done, Lucas, Riley, and I headed to my mother's place to grab our things. She was extremely happy to know that we were going to work everything out.

"Mommy, where's mys stuffs going?" Riley asked as we loaded up.

"It's going to Daddy's house. That's going to be your home now."

"Ise gets to lib with Daddy?" She asked excitedly. "Daddy, Ise gets to lib with you?"

"Yeah, baby girl, and so does your mommy. Would you like that?"

"Yes." She squealed.

"Me too, baby girl, me too." Lucas winked at me as we pulled off and headed to what will now be our home. I'm happy, but I'm nervous too.

"What are you thinking about so hard over there?" Lucas asked. "You good?"

"I'm fine." I smiled at him. "I'm fine. Just thinking about how happy I am even though I'm nervous about this step that we're making."

"We're going to be fine, Amelia. We were made for each other. It just took us a while to figure that out."

"But we're going to be okay, yeah?" He's said it before, but I needed to hear it again. I needed his courage and confidence like I needed to breathe.

"We're going to be more than okay. I love you and I love our daughter. That will never change."

"I love you too."

A few months ago, I would have never guessed that this is the way my relationship with Lucas would be. I'm sure that over time we will have our ups and downs, but we will face them together.

EPILOGUE

Lucas

4 years later

TODAY WAS GOING to be an amazing day. It's the day that I finally asked Amelia to be my wife. It took me a while to get here, and it had nothing to do with me not being sure.

I was sure that I wanted to marry her when we were kids, so I damn sure knew it when we got back together, but I still needed time to let everything settle into place.

We had to work out our issues and it took a while. I needed Amelia to grow a little bit first. For a while she was timid in our relationship. I knew that it was because she didn't want to do anything wrong, but that's not what I wanted. I wanted her to be herself. Mistakes may happen, but that's a part of life.

We finally got into a good place and then I wanted her to be good to herself. I felt like I owed her that much from the sacrifices that she made for Riley.

I wanted her to figure out what she wanted to do in life.

She tried a few things, school and then working, but neither made her happy. She was so used to being everything to Riley that she would be sad when she was away from her.

So, I asked her what she thought about being a stay at home mom. She's always loved to help people and organize. She could stay home with Riley and help my mother with the family charity. That seemed to be the only thing that made her happy when she was away from Riley, helping people.

"Lucas." Amelia burst through my office door at the bank in a panic. I quickly put the velvet box in my desk drawer.

"Yeah, baby. What's wrong?"

"Nothing's wrong." She locked the door. "Well, something is wrong, but it's nothing like that." She started to undress herself. "It's been too long."

"It's been three days." Not that we usually went three days without having sex, but Riley hasn't been sleeping well since we moved into our new house last week.

"The other day doesn't count." She complained. "It was quick and you didn't come."

"I didn't, but you did. I didn't need to come as long as my woman was satisfied."

"It would have satisfied me more if you would have gotten your cum all over me." She started unzipping my pants.

"Fuck, baby. You've gotten very good at being a bad girl." When she was done, she grabbed my hand and pulled me up. Turning around, she bent over my desk and spread her legs.

She needed to be fucked, but she was wide open for me so I bent over and slid my tongue in her already wet pussy. "Ahhh, Lucas." I slowly licked from her opening until I reached her clit. I slowly sucked it into my mouth.

Once I knew that she was wet and ready for me I stood up behind her and sank my cock into her pussy in one thrust.

She moaned...loud. So loud that I reached around and covered her mouth with my hand.

"Looks like this is going to be another quick one, baby. Seems like you can't stay quiet." I whispered to her as I slammed into her harder and harder. It didn't take long before her pussy walls were clenching me.

I was close, so fucking close. "I...I want y-you to come in my m-mouth." Amelia moaned.

"Fuck...fuck. If you want my cum, baby, you better come on because I can't hold it much longer." I eased out of her, and she turned around and fell to her knees.

Grabbing the side of her face as she took my cock into her warm and wet mouth, I pushed in until I could feel her throat and that did it. My cum emptied into her mouth and as the last of it was coming out, I pulled out of her mouth and let it run down her lips and chin. "My mouth."

We cleaned up from our little office quickie in my office bathroom and then she headed off to finish her errands while I finished work.

It was Friday, so as always, we met at my parents' house that evening. She no doubt thought that it was going to be a regular weekend night. We had dinner with everyone and then settled Riley in her grandpa's care since he was still her favorite person in the world. Then it was time to set my plan in motion.

"Let's take a walk, sweetheart." I said to Amelia with my hand stretched out. She took it, blindly allowing me to lead the way and I did, right to our little clubhouse that we made into our pretend home so many years ago.

My younger brothers had done a good job with the instructions I gave them. There were rose petals starting at the edge of the trees going all the way to the clubhouse. When you got closer there were a bunch of twinkling lights hanging down.

Amelia gasped as she looked around. "This is so pretty. You did this?"

"Of course I did. This is our place, remember?" It was for us and only us. When I was a kid I threw such a fit about this being me and Amelia's home and no one else's that my siblings wouldn't even try to come in.

"Why?"

"Because I wanted to ask you to marry me in the place where I first fell in love with you."

Her head whipped around just as I was lowering to my knee. "Amelia, I've loved you for a long time, since I was just a boy. We've had our ups and downs and many chances, but one thing has never changed, me loving you. I've only grown to love you more and more each day. I know it took me a while to get here, but now that I am, I don't want to waste time. I want it to be us, forever and always. Will you marry me, sweetheart?"

She fell into my arms and started to sob while nodding her head. "I need to hear you say it, Amelia. Will you marry me?"

"Yes, Lucas. Yes, I will marry you." She continued to cry. "I…I've got a surprise of my own."

"Oh yeah. What surprise?"

"Riley may finally be getting her baby brother." She started to smile."

"What? You're pregnant?"

"I am. We're going to have another baby, Lucas. Isn't that exciting."

"It sure is. God, I love you, sweetheart."

"I love you too."

ALSO BY MJ MANGO

UNEXPECTED LOVE SERIES

Unleash Me
UnRavel Me
Unbreak Me

UNDYING LOVE SERIES

Fighting Love
Chasing Love

THE WAGNER BOYS SERIES

Meant to Be

THANK YOU

Thank you to each and every one of you that chose to read my book. I'm thankful for every reader.

If this is your first time reading my work, I highly recommend you get started with the **Unexpected Love Series** while waiting for the next one in this series.

I love to connect with readers. I'm on all social media as Author MJ Mango. We would also love to have you in my readers group, **MJ Mango's Heartache Haven.** My group is the first to know about **new releases** and **preorders**.

Catch up with all things MJ Mango at **www.mjmango.com**!!!

Made in the USA
Columbia, SC
18 June 2025

59396737R00083